DRUXEL
MANOR

DRUXEL MANOR

Tarra Young

To order additional copies of this book, contact:
Xlibris Corporation
1-888-795-4274
www.Xlibris.com
Orders@Xlibris.com

This book is dedicated to
my Grandma,
LaVaune George Payne Ames Young.

she was an excellant writer
and I inherited my love for writing from her.

1

It was a cold bleak winter night and the rain was beginning to come down harder. Angel Parker still had another ten miles to drive before she reached the next town and the closest motel.

Angel wished the rain would clear up soon, but it didn't look like it was going to be happening. The rain was pouring down harder by the minute and it was getting harder to see.

As much as Angel hated the decision, she knew she had to pull over to the side of the road. It was now impossible to see the road.

Angel pulled over to the side of the road. She found a napkin in the glove compartment and wiped the windshield with it, but it didn't do much good.

The only thing left for Angel to do was wait for the rain to clear up some so she could see again, but what she really wanted to do was get to the motel as quickly as possible and order out for food before climbing into bed and going to sleep.

Today had been a long day. It all started when she was awakened early this morning by someone knocking on her front door. It was a man delivering a telegram from her brother, telling her to come quick.

Angel's brother Trevor had spent the past six months trying to find their biological parents who had given them up at birth.

Angel had been against looking for their parents, but Trevor would not take no for an answer. Angel feared what the outcome would be if their biological parents were found. She also feared that the couple who had raised the two of them would be hurt in the end.

When Peter and Claudia Parker adopted Angel and Trevor, Angel had only been four months old and Trevor was three years old. Peter and Claudia were the only parents she had ever known.

Angel Shivered as wind whipped against her small compact sized car. Angel checked her watch. It was 11:20 PM. Angel sighed.

Finally by 11:30 PM, the rain let up enough so Angel could see. Angel started her car. When she did, she let out a little gasp.

Through her back window she could make out a car that looked like the same red car she had seen parked in front of her house that morning when she was leaving.

She had convinced herself that the red car she had seen following close behind her couldn't possibly be the same red car, that she was letting her imagination get the best of her. Now she was sure that she was being followed. There was no doubt about it.

Angel pulled back out onto the road. The red car pulled out onto the road behind Angel.

Angel kept an eye on the car behind her through her rear view mirror as she drove.

Angel was relieved when she saw the city limit sign welcoming her to Richmond Heights.

Angel decided she couldn't risk going to the motel with someone following her.

Angel decided the best thing to do was to drive straight to the police station and see if the car continued to follow.

A few minutes later, Angel pulled up in front of the police station near the doors. She was prepared to run inside if the need arose.

Angel watched as the car continued on down the road;. Angel was relieved. She waited a few more minutes before she pulled back out onto the road.

Angel looked all around to make sure they were gone. She let out a sigh of relief when she didn't see the red car anywhere in sight.

It was near midnight and all Angel could think about was getting a bite to eat and getting to the motel and going straight to bed.

Angel looked around for a hamburger joint that had a drive-thru that was still open.

Angel found a place ten minutes later. She ate her food as she drove. Angel was starved. She hadn't had a bite to eat since lunch.

Angel wondered what her brother had discovered about their biological parents that would make him insist that she come to Druxel Manor in Cedar Pines where he was staying.

Angel had almost not made this trip. She still wondered if she had made the right decision.

Angel had called her parents and left a message on their answering machine at their house instead of calling them at work.

She had simply told them that she needed to go out of town for a few days and would be back as soon as she could.

She couldn't bring herself to tell them the truth. The truth was something she could never bring herself to tell them.

She knew they didn't like the idea that Trevor was looking for their biological parents. She could never hurt her parents the way Trevor was hurting them.

As far as Angel was concerned, they were already with their real parents.

It was true that Angel often wondered what their biological parents were like, but she had no real desire to meet them.

Their adoptive parents had done a great job raising them. They had always seen to it that she and Trevor had attended the best schools. They had even paid Angel and Trevor's way through college.

Angel thought about Karen Parker. Karen was one year older than Angel. Karen was the greatest big sister anyone could ever ask for. Karen was Mr. and Mrs. Parker's biological daughter, but they always treated all three children the same.

Angel could not accept anyone else as parents. She was actually glad that their biological parents had given them up for adoption.

"Now why can't Trevor see things the way I do?" Angel thought as she pulled her car into the motel parking lot.

By 12:30 she finally got a room. Angel quickly changed into a warm pair of flannel pajamas.

It felt so good when she wiggled down under the blankets. Within minutes she was sound asleep.

2

Light shined into the room the next morning. Angel yawned and turned over to look at the clock on the stand beside the bed.

Angel gasped. She couldn't believe she had slept that long. It was a quarter to ten.

Angel climbed out of the nice warm bed and rushed into the bathroom to take a quick shower.

After her shower, she came back out and rummaged around in her suitcase until she found a clean pair of jeans and a light pink sweatshirt.

Angel grabbed her comb and her blow dryer out of her suitcase and hurried back into the bathroom.

Thirty minutes later she was ready to get back on the road. Angel grabbed her suitcase , purse, and car keys.

She took one more quick look around the room to make sure she hadn't forgotten anything.

Once she got to her car, she tossed her suitcase into the back seat of her car before getting in.

In a few hours she'd be at Druxel Manor. While Angel waited for her car to warm up, she wondered what key Druxel Manor held to finding their biological parents.

Angel had been worried about Trevor since the day he left. It was her worry for Trevor that had made her decide to start out on this trip to begin with.

Angel backed her car out of the parking place and slowly pulled out onto the road.

Through her rear view mirror, Angel saw a flash of red, as the same red car pulled out behind her. She was being trailed once again.

"This better be very important, Trevor", Angel said out loud to herself.

Whoever was in the red car, they seemed persistent to stay with her.

Angel headed for the nearest gas station. The red car pulled in right behind her.

Angel watched as the car parked. Angel got out of her car to fill her tank. She watched a man who was tall with dark brown hair step out of the car.

The guy was quite handsome. Angel had to admit it. She wondered what the guy could possibly want with her. Angel watched as the guy walked over to the pay phone.

Angel noticed that the guy watched her as he talked. "Who could the man possibly be talking to about her?" Angel wondered.

****

"Don't lose her again," Trevor barked into the phone, "You know how important it is that you stay with her."

"I know, but I'm telling you, she's onto me."

Trevor knew this could be a real problem. He knew how Angel was. If she found out he had hired someone to tail her, she'd probably never speak to her again, even if it was for her own protection. Angel was a strong willed woman and thought she could take care of herself.

"Keep tailing her", Trevor said calmly.

"But what if she really is onto me and she confronts me?"

Trevor thought about it for a moment before speaking. "If she confronts you, you'll just have to think of something, but whatever you do, don't tell her the truth. Angel must not ever find out the truth."

With that, Trevor hung up the phone.

****

The man was just getting back in his car when Angel came out of the gas station after paying for her gas and a breakfast burrito she had grabbed to eat on the road.

As she was pulling out, she looked in her rear view mirror, and sure enough, the handsome man was right behind her.

Angel was no longer as scared of the man as she had been the night before. She realized that if this man wanted to hurt her, he had plenty of chances and didn't.

At that moment, Angel realized that she had forgotten to call her office that morning before leaving the motel to check for messages.

Angel also realized that she had her cell phone in her purse, but had forgotten to turn it on. If anyone had tried to reach her, it would have been impossible.

Angel saw a turn off up ahead of her and decided to take it. When she did, the man in the red car wasn't expecting it. He kept going, until he realized Angel had pulled off.

The man in the red car slammed on his breaks, nearly causing an accident as the cars behind him slammed on their breaks.

Angel laughed and kept going until she found a safe place to pull over to the side of the road.

Angel removed her cell phone from her purse and checked her messages on her cell phone first. She had three messages. Two from her mother and one from her boyfriend, Scott Osborn.

Angel had left in such a hurry the day before that she'd forgotten to call Scott. "Scott must be worried sick about me", she thought.

Angel knew she had to call Scott, but what would she say to him. Scott would never understand.

She also needed to call her parents. She didn't know what to say to them either.

She decided to call her office first. Before Angel could get her office number dialed completely, a black Mercedes Benz pulled up behind her.

Angel froze when a man in a black tuxedo stepped from the car and started walking towards her car.

The guy opened her car door and undid her safety belt before he drug her from the car.

Angel began to kick and scream. The man reached around her and clamped his hand over her mouth.

The man began dragging her toward his car. Angel had never been so scared in her life.

Out of nowhere, the man from the red car appeared. He grabbed Angel's attacker from behind, causing him to release Angel.

Angel fell to the ground and watched in horror as the two men began to fight.

First the man from the red car was on to slugging Angel's attacker over and over in the face. Then Angel's attacker was on top, but not for long. The man from the red car was soon able to get control of the fight again.

Angel's attacker soon fought free. His tuxedo was torn to shreds. He ran to his car and sped off.

The man from the red car ran over and pulled Angel to her feet.

The man then kept a firm grip on her arm. His breath was a bit ragged still from fighting, when he said, "I'm taking you with me.".

3

Angel tried to yank away as she yelled, "Not until you tell me who you are and why you have been following me."

The mans had a strong grip on Angel's wrist and it was impossible for her to break free from it no matter how hard she tried.

"There will be plenty of time for introductions later", the man said as he pulled her around to the passenger side of the car.

He opened the passenger side door and shoved Angel into the front seat. While the man was walking around the car, Angel tried to make her escape.

Before Angel knew it, the man was in the drivers seat and pulled Angel back into the car. The man pulled the door closed and locked all the doors from a control panel on his side of the car. Angel knew she had to face it, there was just no escaping. She was trapped.

"What about my stuff in my car?" Angel demanded to know as the man pulled the car out onto the road.

"I'll send someone for it later."

"You still haven't told me who you are and where are you taking me?"

"Just call me James and don't worry about where I'm taking you," he said as he laughed, "You'll find out in due time, just relax."

"What do you want from me?" Angel asked getting a little irritated.

"I don't want anything from you, I just want you to sit there like a good little girl."

At this point Angel was fuming, but she bit her tongue. How dare this man, that she didn't know, treat her like a child. It was insulting to her.

"My brother is going to be searching for me soon", Angel said hoping that this would persuade the man to let her go.

"No he won't."

"And just how would you know that," Angel demanded, "Do you know my brother?"

"I . . . ."

"Wait a minute, you don't have to answer that," Angel said cutting him off, "You do know my brother., just tell me one thing and I want the truth, "Just how do you know my brother?"

The man hesitated for a minute before he answered, "I work for him."

"You mean he hired you to follow me?"

"Well, it wasn't his main reasoning for hiring me, but I guess you could say he hired me to trail you, but he told me to never let you know."

"Just wait till I get through with the brother of mine."

"He was only trying to look out for you and to protect you."

"I don't need to be looked after or protected. I can't take care of myself just fine."

"Oh yeah, wanna make a bet?" James asked with a grin.

Angel glared at him.

"You didn't seem to be able to take care of yourself back there when one of Jake Taylor's men was stalking you."

"Who's Jake Taylor?"

"I'm not saying."

"Look, I'm in this up to my eyebrows, I have been attacked already, now I demand to know what my brother has gotten me into."

"I have already said too much as it is and I can't risk blowing this case. You'll find out soon enough."

Well, Angel thought to herself, if James was speaking, I'll just wait till we get to Druxel Manor, if that was where James was taking her and get the information out of Trevor.

Angel turned to look at James, "You are taking me to Druxel Manor in Cedar Pines, aren't you?"

"Of course I am. My job is to make sure you get there safe.

Just wait till I have a word with you my dear brother, Angel thought as she leaned back in the seat to get more comfortable. She closed her eyes and pretended to be asleep.

Angel opened her eyes slightly and watched James as he drove. Angel had to admit he was the best looking guy she had ever met in her life.

James had dark brown hair. A few strands of hair had fallen in James' eyes. Angel was tempted to reach over and brush them out of his eyes, but she resisted the temptation.

Angel's mind wondered to her boyfriend, Scott. Scott was attractive in his own way, but Angel had to admit to herself that she was more attracted to James, than she had ever been to Scott.

A pang of guilt shot through Angel at the thought. Then she realized that her purse and cell phone was still in her car and she hadn't had a chance to call him or her parents. They had to be really worried by now.

A tear ran down Angel's cheek as she thought about how hurt and disappointed the people in her life that she loved the most were going to be if they knew what she was doing at this moment while they were worrying about her.

"What's wrong?" James asked with a tenderness in his voice.

"My boyfriend and my parents are probably worried about me by now. They have no idea where I am."

"We'll be at Druxel Manor in less then an hour, you can call them then"

"It's not that simple."

"What do you mean?"

"If they were to ever find out the real reason for this unexpected trip, my parents would be deeply hurt, and my boyfriend Scott would never be able to fully understand why I'm doing this."

"You mean you have never told your adoptive parents about this search?"

"Of course not. My parents would be devastated if they were to ever find out any of this."

"You mean you intend to keep this a secret from them?"

"For as long as I can. I know they'll find out eventually, but I am dreading that day."

"What makes you so certain that your adoptive parents will be upset if you haven't talked to them about this?"

"I just have this awful feeling that the day they find out, they'll feel that they failed us some how."

"Aren't you even the slightest bit curious to about finding out who your biological parents really are?"

"Has Trevor found them?"

""You haven't answered my question."

Angel stared out the window for a few minutes before answering, "Maybe a little bit, but not at the expense of hurting my parents. They were good to me and Trevor while we were growing up."

4

Angel noticed that they had pulled up to a large gate. James honked the horn and the large gate slid open to reveal a long tree lined driveway. At the end of the driveway stood Druxel Manor.

Druxel Manor was larger than Angel had ever envisioned it to be. It was a lovely house, but at the same time, Angel knew that it contained many mysteries.

Angel looked up at the large white columns lining the front of the house. She stepped from the car and looked up at the house in amazement. The house she grew up in was large, but no where near the size of Druxel Manor. Even the property was larger.

Angel knew that whoever owned Druxel Manor had to be loaded with money. Angel jumped at the sound of a man's voice. "So, you've finally returned?"

Angel whirled around to see a man in a grey suit had approached James. "Trevor has asked me to inform you upon your return that he'd like to have a word with you in his office."

"His Office? What office? Why would Trevor have an office here?" Angel wondered. Just what was Trevor up to? Angel was bound and determined to find out.

"Find someone to show Angel to her room." James said.

Angel saw the look the man gave James before James headed inside. "Now what was that look all about?" Angel Wondered. There was definitely something going on and Angel was going to find out what it was.

****

Angel finished washing up and changed into the light blue pants suit that Maria, one of the maids had laid out on the bed for her before leaving the room.

Angel eyed the phone on the night stand. There was a couple of calls she had to make before it got much later. As she was reaching for the receiver, there was a knock on the door.

Angel walked over to the door and opened it. It was another maid. "Mr. Parker has sent me to get you and take you to his office." Angel followed the maid down the long hall and up another fight of stairs.

Angel followed the maid down the hallway a short way. The maid stopped in front of a door and knocked. "Come in", Trevor called through the door.

The entered a large office, with a large desk. Trevor sat behind the large desk. He was speaking to someone on the phone. James was sitting was sitting in a chair across from Trevor.

Trevor pointed to the empty chair and indicated for Angel to take a seat. He then gave a nod in the maid's direction and she left the room. "Call me the instant it's taken care of", Trevor said into the phone before hanging up.

"Now can the two of you please tell me what is going on here?" Angel asked, not even bothering to hide the irritation that she felt.

Trevor ignored her question as if she hadn't even asked it. "I have sent someone to retrieve your car and your belongings. They should be returning with it in a few hours."

Angel exploded. "For the love of God, just tell me what is going on. I have every right to know."

"Look, Angel, it's best that you don't know anything. I feel that James here has given out too much information as it is."

"I don't feel he's given out enough . . . ."

Trevor cut her off before she could finish. "I don't want you contacting anyone, not even our adoptive parents."

Angel shot a dirty look in her brothers direction. It annoyed her how he was now referring to the man and women who had been kind enough to raise them and give them the very best things they could as their adoptive parents. "Can I at least call Scott and let him know that I'm alright?"

"No, you must not call anyone and to see that this is done, I have ordered one of the maids to remove the phone from your room."

Angel became alarmed and was now worried. "You did what?! Angel shouted.

James spoke up for the first time, "It's for your own safety, Angel. Trust me, we're only trying to protect you."

Angel turned to James, Protect me from what?! I don't even know you, so why should I trust you?! Angel was beginning to feel furious.

Trevor continued, "You must never leave Druxel Manor alone no matter what. Either James or I must be with you on all trips outside of Druxel Manor."

"What is this," Angel demanded, "A prison?!

"No, your brother and I are just concerned about your safety and want to protect you any way we can."

"If they expected her to be happy about this," Angel thought to herself, They thought wrong and this is definitely not the end of this conversation. Not by a long shot."

****

Later that evening as Angel, Trevor, and James sat at the dinning room table enjoying their dinner, the door bell rang. A maid hurried off to answer the door.

A few minutes later the maid returned. "Mr. Parker, Mr. Whitman is waiting to speak with you in your study."

Trevor thanked the maid and excused himself from the table.

After Trevor left the room, Angel said to James, "Trevor seems to be enjoying this lifestyle and the power that comes with it."

"It's not what you think it is."

"Oh, it's not. Then why don't you enlighten me and tell me how things really are?"

"You know I'd really like to, but that wouldn't be a very wise decision."

"Or do you just choose not to tell me?"

I wouldn't keep secrets from you, if it wasn't for the fact that your life depends on it."

Does my life really depend on it or is this some kind of game the two of you cooked up?"

Angel knew she wasn't being fair to her brother, but she couldn't help it. Trevor had crossed the line this time.

Trevor returned to the room. "I just got some very disturbing news regarding your car and belongings."

"What is it?", Angel asked.

"When Mr. Whitman arrived where your car was, it was gone.".

5

"Gone? What happened to my car?" Angel demanded.

"Lord only knows," and then motioned for James to follow him, "I need to talk to you privately."

Angel looked at James as he began to rise from his seat at the dinner table, and then at her brother, "Wait just a minute, if this is about my car, don't you think I should have a right to know?"

"Don't worry your pretty little head off about this. We're just going up to my office to discuss some business matters. Nothing you would be interested in." With that, they both walked out of the room.

Angel got up from the dinner table and went into the large living room with the big large TV. screen. She curled up on the sofa and picked up the remote. She flipped through all the channels till she found a local news program.

Angel watched absent minded and only caught bits and pieces of it. Her mind was on other things. She caught enough of the weather forecast to know that there was a storm heading for the Cedar Pines area in the next couple of days.

Angel continued to watch this way until one news report caught her full attention. "The women the police have spent the day looking for, her car was found abandoned at the side of the road. Police say there were signs of a struggle. Police say if any one has seen this women, please give them a call". the reporter was sating as a picture of Angel flashed on the screen. Angel recognized the photo as the one Scott always carried in his wallet.

Now Angel knew without a doubt that Scott and her parents were worried about her. She wished she could call them and let them know that she was safe. She looked around for a phone. She spotted one on a small stand in one corner of the room.

She kept to her feet and hurried over to it. Just as she reached out to take the receiver in her hand, a strong hand reached out and clamped her hand a brought it away from the phone.

Angel turned to see who the hand belonged to. It was James. Angel could feel his breath on her neck. It caused every nerve in her body to tingle. Before she knew it, James had turned her to face him and was kissing her.

At first Angel froze, but the kiss was so intense that she finally gave into it. Her whole mind went blank. James was leading her over to the sofa when Angel heard a sound.

She froze when she heard foot steps on the hardwood floor that let to the living room. She quickly pulled away just as Trevor walked into the room.

Angel's mind was spinning and her legs felt like they'd give way any minute if she didn't sit down. Angel made her way over to the sofa and sat down.

Trevor looked at James and then over at Angel. Did I interrupt something?' He asked

James and Angel both said no at the same time and a bit too

quickly. Trevor shot them both a strange look and then shrugged his shoulders.

Reality began to sink in as Angel glanced over at the TV. that was still on. She remembered the news report she'd seen on TV. "Should I tell them," She wondered, "Or did they already know. Could this have been what the secret meeting Trevor and James had in Trevor's office? Or was it about the something else."

Angel thought for a moment and decided she must tell them weather they knew about it or not. Angel turned and looked at Trevor. "I know what happened to my car", Angel said in almost a whisper.

Trevor turned and looked at James. So they did know, Angel thought, So that's what the secret meeting was about and they were going to keep it fro her. Angel found her voice and spoke up, "James didn't tell me."

"Then how did you find out?" Trevor asked.

"It was on the news, they're looking for me."

"Well they won't find you here."

"Trevor, we have to call mom and dad, and Scott."

"No, it's too risky."

"Trevor's right." James said.

"No, he isn't right. We need to call and let them know I'm alright so they'll call off the search."

"As I said before, it's too risky", Trevor said holding his ground.

Angel had to admit, her brother was suborn at times and this was one of them. "What is so risky about it?"

"We can't tell you", Trevor said.

"More secrets. I'm getting sick of all these secrets."

"It's for your own good." James said.

"Why can't I be the judge of that?"

James turned and looked at Trevor. Trevor just shook his head and walked out of the room.

"About what happened before your brother walked in . . ."

"Forget about it. As far as I'm concerned it never happened and it won't happen again." Angel said as she turned and walked out of the room.

"That's just what I was going to say", James called after her.

****

Angel headed straight to her room. She was furious at both Trevor and James. She couldn't figure out though, who she was more mad at. She was mad at Trevor and James for keeping secrets.

She was angry at Trevor for the fact that he was her brother and had pulled her into this mess. She was angry at James for kissing her. She felt used and betrayed because James knew about Scott and he kissed her anyway. But on the other hand, she was angry at herself for giving in to the kiss.

She had to admit that it was the best kiss she ever had. It had left her weak in the knees and wanting more. April felt a pang of guilt as she realized that at that moment she would have gone a lot further than kissing James if Trevor hadn't walked in.

She had betrayed Scott. He trusted her and she had allowed James to kiss her. Why hadn't she shoved him away? she wondered. She couldn't allow it to happen again. She couldn't hurt Scott that way. It was bad enough she had caused Scott to worry about her by not calling him before she left.

Angel realized it was her fault that Scott and her parents were worrying about her. She had plenty of chances to call them and hadn't. In the end her parents and Scott were going to be hurt and it was her fault.

This realization though still didn't lessen the anger she felt towards Trevor and James. Trevor didn't even seem to care that they were causing his parents stress.

Angel realized she hadn't even called her office. If she didn't convince Trevor to let her use the phone soon to at least call her office, she'd be lucky if she had a job when she returned. Angel had worked hard to get the job she had and she wasn't about to mess it up for no one.

Angel found a pink flannel night gown in the dresser drawer. She slipped out of her clothes and pulled the night gown over her head. Once she was in bed, she realized she was more tired then she'd thought. She drifted off to sleep just seconds after her head hit the pillow.

6

The next morning Angel awoke to the sound of howling wind and the windows rattling. She rolled over to look at the digital clock on her nightstand. It was 8:14 Am.

Angel climbed out of bed and headed straight for her private bathroom. She adjusted the water till it was just right before stepping in. The warm water running over her body felt great.

As much as she hated not being able to leave Druxel Manor, it felt great not to have to rush her shower for a change. It felt good just to relax and let the water run over her.

Angel reached for the bottle of shampoo, which turned out to be strawberry scented. After she washed her hair real good, she reached for the bar of soap, which turned out to be the exact same brand she used. Leave it to Trevor, she thought, to remember the small details.

As soon as April finished her shower she stepped out and headed back into her bedroom. The thick white carpet felt great beneath her feet. She headed right for the closet in search of something more comfortable to wear then the outfit she had worn the day before.

In the back of the closet, she found some jeans and took a pair out. Then she found a jade colored blouse to wear with the jeans. In the dresser drawer she found a pair of underwear and a bra. In another drawer she found a pair of jade colored socks to match the blouse. Then it was time to find a pair of shoes to go with her outfit. She settled for a comfortable pair of sneakers.

By the time Angel gathered her outfit, she was beginning to feel a bit cold, so she quickly dressed. Next she headed for the vanity table and sat down on the little chair.

She found a fancy comb and brush. In the drawer she found all kinds of hair accessories. Angel found a jade scrunchy that matched her outfit perfectly. She brushed her hair and then pulled her hair into a ponytail.

Next she applied her make up. Then she sprayed some rose scented perfume from the bottle that was sitting on the vanity table. It was now 9:45. Angel stood and walked over to the full length mirror to see how she looked before leaving the room.

The storm was still going on when Angel left her room. When Angel got to the kitchen, she found an older women in a maid uniform at the sink. When Angel entered the room, she turned to Angel and smiled. "You must be Angel. I have heard so much about you. It's good to finally meet you."

"Thank you", Angel said blushing.

"Why don't you have a seat at the table, and I'll get your breakfast."

"Just coffee and toast for me", Angel said.

"Nonsense," She said, "I'm going to fix you bacon and eggs to put some meet on those bones. You are far too thin," She said as she turned to the refrigerator and got out the bacon and eggs, "By the way, my name Claira."

"Well, hello Claira, it's so nice to meet you", Angel said and she meant it. Claira seemed like one of the nicest women she had ever met. Angel wondered how much information Claira knew.

Just as Claira was sitting a glass of fresh squeezed orange juice and a cup of coffee down in front of her, James walked in. Angel blushed as she remembered the kiss they had shared the night before.

He smiled in Angel's direction as he took a seat at the table. "Could I please get a cup of coffee, Claira?"

"You sure can, Claira said as she got another coffee from the cupboard and poured another cup of coffee. As she sat it down in front of James he thanked her. Angel was relieved when James picked up a newspaper that was laying on the table and began reading it.

A few minutes later, Claira brought Angel her breakfast and went back to finish up the dishes she was washing. There was a dishwasher, but Angel noticed Claira didn't use it and wondered why.

Angel ate her breakfast in silence. When Angel was finishing her breakfast, she looked up to see that Claira had left the room. She was alone with James.

Angel hurried and pushed herself away from the table and began to walk away, when she felt a strong grip on her wrist. She turned and came face to face with James.

"Good morning beautiful", he said as he pulled her into his arms and kissed her again. Angel tried to pull away, but once she felt that same tingle spread through her body that she had felt the night before, she quit fighting it and gave in.

His lips were soft against her and awakened every nerve in her body. When the kiss ended, Angel was week in the knees and was trembling in James' arms. Then reality set in and she could see Scott in her mind. She had betrayed Scott once again and tears ran down her face.

"What's wrong," James asked, "I have seen many reactions from women I have kissed, but never this, so what's the tears for?"

"How can you kiss me like that when you know I have a boyfriend?"

"You don't love Scott", James said.

Angel became defensive. "How can you say that? You don't know how I feel about Scott."

"You're wrong."

"What do you mean?"

"When you talk about Scott, I can see it in your eyes that you don't love him. You don't have that sparkle in your eyes a young woman gets when she's in love."

Angel began to sob because she realized James was right. James pulled her back into his arms to comfort her, but Angel pushed him away and ran out of the room. She needed to be alone to think and sort out her feelings.

7

Angel ran, not knowing where she was going. The tears fell freely. She had vowed to Scott that she'd love him forever and that she wouldn't let anything come between them. Now, unexpectedly she had managed to allow someone to come between them, and that someone had pointed out to her that she didn't love Scott.

Why couldn't she have seen that. Angel came to some large double doors at the end of the hall she had been running down. She opened the door and walked in. She found herself standing in a large library. There rolls and rolls of shelves containing books. It was like a dream. come true. Angel had spent a large portion of her childhood with her nose in a book.

Angel walked along one self running her index finger across the spines of the books as she read the titles of the books. Angel was even more curious now as to who Druxal Manor belonged to. Whoever the owner was, they had great taste in books. Since she had gotten here, Trevor had seemed to be the only one giving the orders. Angel stopped when she came to a book titled "Love Never Forgotten", and pulled it down from the shelf.

Angel looked around. She spotted a large tan leather sofa in the middle of the room with two matching chairs, one on each side of the sofa. Across from it, was a large rock fire place. On the round table in front of the sofa sat a half eaten donut and an empty coffee cup. Whoever it was, they were gone now. Angel found herself wondering if the half eaten donut belonged to James, but quickly pushed the thought to the back of her mind as she sat down to read the book.

But no matter how hard Angel tried to enjoy the book, she just couldn't. Her mind kept wondering back to James. The two kisses they had shared in less then 24 hours of knowing each other. And most importantly, the realization that she didn't love Scott the way she had always thought she did. Angel wondered just what her feelings for James were. She knew she felt something, but what? It couldn't be love. She had just met James. Or could it be? Angel's feelings were to mixed to figure it out.

Angel heard a noise and froze to listen. She could hear movement behind some shelves just a few rows from where she was sitting. She heard Trevor's voice. He was talking to someone, but to who she didn't know. She strained to hear what Trevor was saying. His words were a bit muffled, but she could still make out a little of what he was saying.

"I'm not ready for Angel to find out what happened to our biological parents and the role our adoptive parents had in it, but in the end, whatever does happen, I do not want her near our adoptive parents ever again, go I make myself clear?" "Yes", another man answered. Angel did not recognize his voice. Angel heard a shuffling sound and the door open and close, then some more shuffling and the opened and closed again. Both of them had left the library.

Angel was relieved to be alone. What was Trevor talking about? What is he hiding from me? Angel wondered aloud. Angel's mind was made up. No matter what it took, Angel was going to find out. Angel placed the book back on the shelf where she had found it. She went to the door and opened it, looking both ways before she stepped out into the hall.

Angel hurried as quick as she could. Just as she got to the bottom of the steps, Trevor was coming down the stairs. "There you are, I was worried when I couldn't find you in your room, where have you been?"

"I was looking for you." Angel felt guilty for lying to Trevor, but she wasn't ready to let Trevor know that she had been in the library and heard what he had said.

"You were, was there something you needed?"

"Yes," Angel said remembering she had to call her office, "I need to call my office Trevor and as soon as possible."

"Gee, I don't know . . . ."

"Trevor, I have worked to hard to get where I am in my career to lose it now by not showing up to work and not calling in."

"Oh, alright! But what are you going to tell them?"

"I'm just going to tell them I had a family emergency and will be back into work as soon as I possibly can"

"Okay, I'll let you make the call from my office but make it quick!"

"Thank you Trevor, I owe you one."

Angel followed Trevor up the two flights of stairs and to his office. Trevor stepped into the office and sat down at his desk, "Now remember, make it quick."

"I will, don't worry about it", Angel said as she picked up the phone and punched in the number to her office.

On the third ring, her boss, Harold answered the phone.

"Angel, Where are you?" Harold demanded.

Angel glanced in Trevor's direction before responding, "I can't tell you that now, all I can tell you is I'm safe."

"Do realize that you parents have been calling here worried sick about you and your photo has been plastered all over the news?"

"Yes."

"And you haven't bothered to call and let anyone know you're alright? You better have a good explanation for this."

Angel glanced in Trevor's direction again. She remembered the conversation she had heard in the library. "Harold, I'm on a lead. I think I have the lead on a story that could make the front page of the paper." Trevor shot her a questioningly look.

"Well I trust your opinion, but what should I tell your parents?"

"Just tell them I'm alright and that I'm on an assignment and will be home as soon as I can." Angel noticed the look Trevor was giving her. She quickly said goodbye and hung up the phone.

8

Later that day Angel went back to the library and retrieved the book she had been trying to read earlier and headed up to her room with it. She was laying on her bed now staring at the cover of the book. "Love Not Forgotten" she read aloud.

Her mind returned to the kiss she and James had shared that morning and the hurtful words he had said. James was being honest though. In the short time he had known Angel, he seemed to know her better then she knew herself.

There was another clap of thunder and then a crackling sound and the lights went out. Either the storm had knocked a power line down or a fuse had blown. Angel walked out into the hall in search of Trevor.

She walked only a few feet from her room when someone came up behind her and grabbed her. Angel screamed as loud as she could. Whoever grabbed her was dragging her down the stairs.

Once they reached the bottom of the stairs Angel heard a loud thump and the sound of glass breaking. Whoever had grabbed her released her and she fell to the floor.

Angel looked up and there was a flash of light. She looked up to see a beam from a flashlight shinning on her. A hand reached out to help her up and she heard a failure voice say, "Don't worry, it's me, James.

Angel reached out and took hold of his hand. James pulled her to her feet. "Are you alright?" James asked as he pulled her into his embrace.

"What happened?" Angel asked. James turned the flashlight over to where the man who had grabbed her was laying on the floor. Angel could make out the pieces of glass that she recognized as the vase that sat on the table in the foyer by the front entrance. Angel also recognized the man as the same man who had attacked her the day before.

James had saved her again. Angel wrapped her arms around James and hugged him. She realized she had overreacted earlier to his kiss and the comment he had made. He was only being honest. While in his arms Angel realized it might be worth giving James a chance and exploring whatever it was she was feeling towards James.

At that moment the lights came back on and Angel could hear Trevor calling her name. Angel pulled away from James and they both went towards the back of the house. Trevor had just came in through the back door drenched from head to foot.

"Are you Okay?" Trevor asked as soon as he saw Angel. I heard you scream right after the power went out.

"I'm fine, just a little shaken up, that's all."

"What happened, why did you scream?"

Angel told Trevor everything that had taken place after the power went out.

Trevor looked at James and asked, "was it one of Jake Taylor's men?"

"yes, the same one who attacked her yesterday on her way here."

"And you say you knocked him out?"

"Yes, he was still knocked out cold when we left, I think it'll be a few more minutes before he wakes up, so if we hurry, we should be able to put a stop to the damage he's been doing for Jake."

"That explains why all the breakers were flipped."

There was that name again, Angel thought. She had to find out who he was, but before she could say anything they were heading to the front part of the house.

Angel decided to follow them. When they got there, the man was gone and the front door was left wide open. "Damn it," Trevor yelled as he slammed the front door closed, "We could have had him this time." Without another word Trevor left the room and headed in the direction of his office.

Once again, Angel found herself alone with James. "Can we talk?"

"Sure", Angel said as James took her by the hand and led her into the living room.

"I think it's time you and I faced the truth about how we feel about one another."

"So do I," Angel said, "And I'm willing to explore whatever it is we are feeling for each other."

"You are?" James sounded shocked.

"Sure", Angel said.

James took Angel into his arms and kissed her. This time Angel didn't fight the kiss, but gave into it freely. This kiss seemed far more deeper than the other two kisses and was filled with a strong passion that Angel had never felt before. It seemed to awaken every nerve in Angel's body and she felt emotions she had never experienced before in her life.

James pulled away and rose to his feet. He reached out with both hands and when Angel placed her hands in his, he pulled her to her feet. In one swift movement, he lifted Angel into his arms and carried her up the stairs and took her into a room a few doors down from her own bedroom, which turned out to be his bedroom.

James kissed her once again before he gently lay laid her down on his bed. James laid down beside her on the bed and continued kissing her. He then dropped lower and kissed her neck.

He trailed Sweet genital kisses up and down her neck. Angel pressed against him. She couldn't seem to get close enough to him.

James ran his finger down Angel's neck to the top of her blouse and slowly unbuttoned it. Soon Angel could feel cool air on her skin that was beaded with sweat.

James cupped her left breast with his right hand. Angel could feel the heat coming from James through the lace of her bra and it sent wonderful sensations through her body. Angel Moaned.

Angel had to feel James flesh against hers, so she began to pull at his shirt. James realized what she was trying to do and slipped it over his head. James rolled on top of Angel. She could feel the heat between them as their flesh touched and moaned again.

James slipped one bra strap down and then the other. He pulled her bra down and freed both breasts. Then he cupped her breasts, one in each hand. Then he released them. He lowered his head and began to suck on one nipple and then the other.

The sensations going through Angel were maddening. She to have him in her. "Make love to me she moaned."

"Not yet," James said as he slowly began trailing kisses down her stomach and then back up to her neck, "I want to take this nice and slow". . He then worked his way back down to her breasts and suckled on one nipple then the other.

Angel wiggled in anticipation beneath him. Once again he trailed kisses down her stomach, but this time, when he got to the waist band of her jeans, he stopped and undid her jeans and slowly slid them off from her as he kneeled over her. James took off his own jeans and underwear next. Angel couldn't help, but look down at his hardness. James then slowly slid her underwear off. Angel was now fully exposed.

James slid two fingers into her hot, moist spot and began to massage her there. Angel arched her back as she pressed closer to him. Without warning, James tongue replaced his fingers. Angel was moaning with desire. Just when she thought she was going to explode, with one swift movement, James was in her. Within minutes they were both moaning in pure ecstasy.

9

Angel and James Lay in each others arms, exhausted and drenched in sweat. After fifteen minutes of rest, the made love once more and then they both fell asleep.

Angel awoke a few hours later. She hadn't even realized she had fallen asleep. Then a terrible thought crossed her mind. What if Trevor had come looking for them. If he checked her room and she wasn't there and if he looked for James and couldn't find him, he might put two and two together and figure out she was with James, or he might even become worried and think that awful man had come back and got her.

Worrying Trevor was the last thing she wanted to do, it was bad enough she was worrying her parents and Scott . . . . Scott, she hadn't thought about him all afternoon. She quickly pushed the thought to the of her mind and slipped out of bed and without waking James and searched for her clothes.

She grabbed the sheet that was laying in a heap at the bottom of the bed and quickly wrapped it around her. She slowly opened the door and looked both ways before going out into the door. Angel turned and closed the door quietly behind her.

She turned to make a quick dash to her room and gasped. "Trev . . . .", she began then stopped. It wasn't Trevor, only a man who looked a lot like Trevor. So much that they could pass a twins.

"I'm so sorry, I didn't mean to startle you." He said.

Angel was startled, but tried not to show it. She recognized his voice. He was the same man Angel had over heard Trevor talking to in the library that morning. This man knew a lot and Angel wished she could find out what he knew without letting on she was in the library, but she knew that was impossible.

Instead she said "Excuse me", and headed straight for her room. She was relieved when the door was closed behind her. Could it be possible that man was Trevor's twin? Did Trevor even have a twin brother? It was time for her to get to the bottom of things. She hated the idea of spying on Trevor, but it was the only way.

Angel dropped the sheet to the floor and went in and took a quick shower. She put on a clean pair of jeans and a blouse. She quickly pulled her hair into a ponytail before going down stairs. She could hear Trevor talking to the man that looked like him. As soon as Angel entered the room, they stopped talking.

Trevor looked in Angel's direction with a displeased look on his face. Then he turned to the man standing next to him, "Angel, this is a friend of mine. His name is Dave."

Angel could tell he was lying. Angel turned to face her brother's look-a-like, "Nice to meet you."

James entered the room and their eyes met across the room for a short moment, then James turned and looked in Trevor's direction. Angel looked over at her brother. He looked angry and his eyes were fixed piercingly on James.

"James, in the library now, we need to talk." Trevor said.

James looked over at Angel one last time before he followed Trevor out of the room.

"You'll have to excuse me", Dave said as he went the opposite direction as Trevor and James.

Angel waited till Dave was out of sight before heading in the direction of the library, As much as she hated the idea, she knew if she was going to find out anything, she needed to spy on them.

Angel walked into the library and saw them sitting on the sofa. She hid behind a shelf not far from where they were to listen. "when I told you to distract Angel, I didn't mean for you to have sex with you. That's not what I'm paying you for.

So that's why James has been coming onto me, she thought. He had been lying to her the whole time. Tears began to fall down Angel's face. She turned to leave the room and knocked a stack of books to the floor.

In an instant, Angel heard James call out her name and he was by her side. "You're crying ," he said, trying to wipe the tears away, "It's not what you think", he said as he tried to hug her.

Angel shoved him out of the way and ran out of the library. She had to leave. She couldn't stay here a moment longer. She ran into the living room.

Before James could stop her, she was on the phone with a local cab company. As soon as she hung up, James was by her side. "Angel, please don't do this. I can explain if you'll just give me a chance.

"Save it for someone who's stupid enough to believe your lies", Angel snapped.

"Angel, I love you."

"I don't want to hear it." Angel said as she headed for the front door.

"Where are you going? It's pouring down rain out there."

"Where I go and what I do is no longer your concern."

"I said I can explain that . . . ."

"And I told you I don't want to hear it", April said. She opened the door and stepped out into the rain, slamming the door behind her. James opened the door and followed her out into the rain.

A few minutes later, Trevor came out. "Angel, come back inside."

"No, I'm getting sick and tired of you treating me like a baby and hiring James to baby sit me."

"That's not how it is", James said.

"You are making a big mistake by leaving."

"No Trevor, the biggest mistake I made was coming here, leaving here is the best decision I have made in days. I'm tired of all the secrets and the lies you both told."

"We can explain it all if you'll just give us a chance. It was my decision to keep it from you. James wanted to tell you, but I told him no."

"It still doesn't excuse the fact that James had sex with me, just to distract me from what is really going on."

"That's not why I made love to you, Angel"

"Please come inside so we can discuss this where it is warm and dry."

"It'll be warm and dry in the Taxi."

"Now you're being ridiculous!" Trevor shouted.

Angel was relieved when the Taxi pulled up. She had the back door open and was getting in before the driver could step out of the Taxi.

"Please don't do this," James pleaded, "Please stay. I know we can work out some sort of an agreement if you'd just give me half a chance."

Angel closed the door and locked it without responding to James' pleas. James had hurt her more then any man ever had. There was no working things out. To give him a chance would just be giving him the chance to hurt her again.

"Where to?" the driver asked.

Angel gave the cab driver her address. This was going to be the most expensive taxi ride Angel had ever taken, but she felt it would be well worth it.

Angel closed her eyes and breathed a sigh of relief once they pulled away from Druxel Manor.

10

As the cab pulled up in front of Angel's apartment building, she never thought she'd be as happy as she was now to be back home.

After explaining to the cab driver that she needed to go in and get her check book to pay the cab fare, she stepped out of the cab and hurried quickly inside.

Once she got to her front door, she realized she didn't have her key. This meant she had to pay her landlady, Mrs. Hayes, a visit. Mrs. Hayes loved to talk and this meant that her cab fare was going to go up even more.

Once Mrs. Hayes got going on a subject, she could talk for hours. Angel had to come up with a quick plan. Angel knocked on Mrs. Hayes door and waited.

A few minutes later she came to the door. Before Mrs. Hayes had a chance to speak, Angel said, "I haven't got much time and I haven't got my key and I was wondering if you could help me get into my apartment."

"Why of course, hon, just give me a moment to get my key."

Angel could just imagine what the taxi meter was up to now as she waited. She could hear Mrs. Hayes rummaging around through things before she reappeared a few moments later with the key.

Mrs. Hayes handed Angel the key and before Angel could turn and go, Mrs. Hayes said, "You know you had a lot of people worried about you dear. Where have you been?"

"I was covering a story", Angel said. She hated lying, but didn't feel she should tell the truth.

"Oh, so I can expect to read another one of your amazing stories in the paper in a day or two?"

"Um . . . It didn't pan out", Angel said.

"That's really to bad dear."

"Yes it is, but really have to be going now", Angel said as she hurried off in the direction of her apartment. On some occasions she really enjoyed talking to Mrs. Hayes, but today was not one of them, especially when it was costing her money.

It seemed good to be home. Angel wanted get the cab driver paid, then all ties to Druxel Manor would be cut once and for all.

Angel got her front door open and when she did, she gasped. Someone had ransacked her apartment. Angel checked her door for any sign of a break in and could not find one. She then went through her apartment and checked all the windows. None of them were broke and everything seemed secure.

"That's odd," She thought, "Whoever had broken in had to have a key, but who?"

The only people who had a key to her apartment besides herself were Mrs. Hayes, her parents and Scott and Angel doubted very much that one of them would wreak her apartment this way.

Angel remembered the cab driver was still waiting and rushed to the kitchen to get her key to her desk in her office. Whoever did this to her apartment had skipped over her office. Angel quickly grabbed an in pen and her check book went out to pay the cab driver.

When she came back in, shut and locked her door. She wondered if maybe the police had done this to her apartment. Angel decided to find out for sure.

She walked into her office and dialed Scott's office number. After the third ring he answered.

"It's me."

"Thank God, we have all been worried sick, where are you?"

"I'm home now."

"Where were you ?"

"I was working on a story, but it fell through, so now I'm back."

"Why didn't you tell anyone you were leaving and why didn't you call us?"

"It all came up so unexpectedly, I guess I forgot."

"That still doesn't explain why you didn't the whole time you were gone."

Angel felt he was giving her the third degree, so she did her best to change the subject. "Do we have to talk about this now?"

"Isn't this as good a time as any?"

"It's not why I called."

"Then why did you call?"

"Did the police search my apartment at any time while I was away?"

"No, what makes you ask that?"

"When I got home this afternoon, I noticed that my apartment had been trashed like someone had been looking for something."

"Oh my God, Angel, just hold tight, I'll be there in about ten minutes."

"That isn't necessary . . ."

"What do you mean it isn't necessary? I'll be there in ten minutes", Scott said before he hung up the phone.

Great, Angel thought as she stared at the receiver. She wasn't even sure she was ready to face Scott just yet. She hoped he never found out about James and what went on between them.

Angel hung up the receiver, then picked up the receiver and looked at the receiver once again while she debated if she should call the police or not. Nothing appeared to be missing, but to be on the safe side, she decided to give them a call.

Angel's plans for the afternoon were shot. She had planned on coming home and grabbing a quick bite to eat and then going right to bed. She hadn't gotten much sleep in the Taxi on the way home. All she could think about was how James had hurt her.

Angel went into the living room to wait. A few moments later, Scott arrived. "Does anything seem to be missing?" he asked.

"No, that's the strange part. This couldn't have been just a random robbery, that's why I called the police."

"You called the police! Why did you do that?"

Scott sounded upset, but Angel couldn't figure out why. "I just felt the safest thing to do was get the police involved in case whoever did this decides to come back."

"That, makes sense, I guess."

Scott didn't sound to sincere in what he was saying. Angel wondered what his problem was. Why was he so against her calling the police? What did Scott have to hide? Maybe she was imagining things. She had to be.

11

Two hours later, Angel was showing the police out. They had taken a police report and said they would call if they found out anything.

Angel walked into the kitchen and began rummaging around in the refrigerator for something to eat. The only problem was everything had to be and the kitchen was a mess.

"Why don't we just go out for dinner tonight?" Scott said coming up behind her, "Then you can spend the night at my house."

Angel was not fond of the idea of spending the night with Scott, but what choice did she have? It would take hours to get in room back in order and she was too tired to clean it tonight.

Scott put his arm around her and led her out of the apartment. I may not love Scott, Angel thought, but at least he had never hurt her the way James had and she doubted he ever would.

"Where would you like to eat?" Scott asked once they were in the car.

"Can we just go straight to your place and order a pizza?"

"Whatever you'd like", Scott said as he started the car."

Once they reached Scott's, he called for a pizza to be delivered before he sat down on the sofa next to Angel.

He slipped his arm around Angel and pulled her too him and Angel laid her head down on his shoulder. "So where were you?" Scott asked, "It's just not like you to disappear and not call?"

Angel lifted her head up and looked up at Scott, "Do we have to talk about this now?"

"Why, isn't right now a good enough time to discuss this?"

"No, it's not."

"Why not, Angel? When is it going to be a good time?"

"Come on, Scott," Angel said in an irritated tone, then added in more calmly, "I'm just tired."

"Okay, I understand", Scott said and dropped the subject.

Angel wondered how long she could keep avoiding the topic. Angel hated keeping secrets from Scott, but she didn't know how he'd be able to handle knowing where she had gone.

She knew the truth would hurt her parents too. She realized she hadn't contacted them since she got back in town. She reached for Scott's cell phone on the coffee table and dialed the number.

"Hello?"

"Hi mom"

"Angel dear, where are you? We've been so worried about you."

"I'm back mom, I'm sorry I worried you. I never meant to worry you and dad that way."

"I know dear, you would never do anything to purposely worry us, her mother said, "Where are you? You're not in danger are you?"

"No mom, I'm back in town. Right now I'm over at Scott's."

"Oh good, now I don't have to worry about you. I'm sure Scott will take really good care of you."

"Yes he will, mom."

Angel and her mother said their goodbyes and Angel hung the phone up. She was relieved her mother hadn't asked where she had been. Angel knew it would only be a matter of time and her mother would be wanting to know where she had been and so would her father. She knew it was a question she wouldn't be able to keep dodging forever.

The pizza finally arrived. Angel could only eat two slices because she was so tired. She turned to Scott, "I think I'm going to turn in for the night."

"I'll come with you", Scott said as he kissed her and slipped his hand in her blouse and rubbed her breasts. An image of James popped into Angel's mind. She felt guilty. Angel pushed Scott away. "Not tonight, Honey", she said as she walked away, "I'm too tired."

****

Angel laid in bed thinking. How long would she be able to keep her secret and how long would she be able to push Scott away before he realized what was going on and that there was another man? That was the last thing Angel Wanted.

Angel needed to decide quickly if she wanted to continue her relationship with Scott or if she wanted to move on. She knew it wasn't fair to Scott she were to lead him on. Her relationship with Scott was comfortable, just the way she liked it. Maybe she really did love Scott. James had probably said what he did to confuse her so he could take advantage of her.

Scott entered the room and began changing into his pajamas. Angel lay silently watching him. She decided then to stay with Scott. He would never hurt her.

Angel waited until Scott laid down before she spoke. "Can we talk?"

Scott jumped and looked at her with a startled look on his face. "Sure, but I thought you were asleep."

"I was just doing a lot of thinking and couldn't sleep."

"Oh, what did you want to talk about?"

"Druxel Manor." Angel said. She saw a look cross Scott's face she had never seen before. It was an angry expression that scared Angel, but left his face just as it had appeared.

"Druxel Manor? What is Druxel Manor?"

"A house, well actually it's a mansion."

"Well, what about Druxel Manor? What is your connection to it?"

"It's where I was." Angel saw that same angry look cross Scott's face and then disappear. She wondered if Scott knew something he wasn't telling.

"Just where is this Druxel Manor?"

"Where it is isn't the important thing."

"Then could you kindly tell what the important thing is?"

"The reason I went is what's most important."

"Then tell me why you went to Druxel Manor?"

"Trevor sent for me."

"I should have known that brother of your's was behind all this," Scott said, "So did you learn anything about your biological parents while you were there?"

"Not really."

"What do you mean by that?"

"Well, the truth is, I came home because Trevor was keeping too many secrets from me?"

"You mean he got you there and then wouldn't tell you anything? I always thought that guy was strange."

"I did get attacked a couple of times while I was there."

"Attacked! Who attacked you?"

"Some man in a tuxedo. He supposedly works for a guy named Jake Taylor."

A look of shock, then anger quickly passed over Scott's face.

"Scott, do you know Jake Taylor?"

"Uhh . . . no, I don't, but why did he attack you?"

"That's one of Trevor's many secrets."

It figures. He gets you into this mess, then won't tell you what's going on."

Scott had never liked Trevor from the day they met, but Angel could never figure out why.

12

The next morning Angel woke up in Scott's arms. She felt guilty because she had been dreaming that she was making love to James.

She had to put all that out of her mind. She needed to forget that any of that had ever happened. She turned over and watched Scott sleep.

Watching Scott sleep was one of the things she had always loved doing. He reminded her of a little boy the way his hair fell over his eyes.

Angel gently reached up to brush the hair out of his eyes. She tried her hardest not to wake him up while doing this, but wasn't very successful.

Scott reached up and grabbed her wrist and pinned her to the bed before kissing her on the lips. He soon and kissed her tenderly on the lips. Soon he was kissing her up and down her neck.

He slid her nightgown over her head and then began trailing kisses up and down her body. An image of James popped into Angel's mind, but she pushed it away.

Scott stopped what he was doing long enough to get a condom out of the drawer. He opened it and laid it on the night stand before continuing any further. Angel knew without a doubt what his intentions were.

Angel was powerless to stop him. She had run out of excuses. She could no longer claim she was tired and if she claimed to have headache, her intentions would be too obvious.

when it was all over with, Angel began to feel guilty. In a way she felt like she had just betrayed James. Like she had just cheated on him.

But how could it be cheating when she wasn't having a relationship with James? She asked herself. She was supposed to be having a relationship with Scott.

Angel waited until Scott had finished his shower and was back in the room dressing before she slipped into the bathroom to take a shower.

Once she was in the shower, that's when she let the tears fall. Angel felt more confused at that moment then she had ever felt in her life, but she knew she had no one to blame but herself for feeling that way.

If she hadn't given into James, she wouldn't be feeling this way now. I should have ignored James she told herself as she stepped into the shower.

Once she was in the shower, that's when she let the tears fall. In a way, Trevor was to blame for all of this as well. If he hadn't interfered in her life by sending her a telegram to go there, then hiring someone to baby sit her, none of this would have ever happened.

Angel let the water slide down her as the tears fell. Her life had seemed so perfect before that telegram and before James had entered her life. Angel cried harder as she realized that in the short time she'd known James, she had fallen in love with him.

Why can't I just love Scott? Angel asked herself. Scott was the type of guy who would never do anything to hurt her the way James had. Angel felt deep down that she deserved how she was feeling now.

Angel shut off the water and stepped out of the shower. She grabbed a towel and dried off before leaving the bathroom. When she got back to the bedroom, Scott was no where around.

Angel found a note on her pillow and opened it and read it.

Hon,

I had to get to the office.
We have a meeting this morning that I forgot about.
You were wonderful this morning.
I'm looking forward to seeing you tonight.

Love Always,
Scott

Angel folded the note back up and laid it on the bed. She remembered a time when a note like that from Scott made her feel special. Now she felt nothing.

This isn't going to work after all, Angel thought to herself. The only solution was going to be breaking it off with Scott. As much as she didn't want to hurt Scott, she couldn't keep leading Scott on this way. She had to tell him tonight.

Angel picked up the phone and called a cab. Then she quickly put on her clothes. She needed to get back to her apartment and get it cleaned up and check for anything that could be missing.

****

Angel had just thanked the cab driver and paid him and he was pulling away when Mrs. Hayes came out. This is all I need, Angel thought, another one of Mrs. Hayes' long stories.

Angel smiled and tried to sound as friendly as possible. "Hi, Mrs. Hayes, how are you today?"

"I'm fine dear, but you had a gentleman caller last night after you left here last night."

"W-w-who was it?" Angel asked stuttering. It couldn't have been Trevor. Mrs. Hayes knew Trevor. Could it have been James? Angel wondered to herself.

"He didn't leave his name."

This wasn't helping Angel at all. "Mrs. Hayes, what did the man look like?"

"He was tall and he had on a tuxedo."

So it wasn't James. Angel didn't know why, but she felt disappointed. She knew who the man was though. It was the man who had attacked her twice.

Angel did not like the idea that the man who had attacked her and tried to take her on more then one occasion knew where she lived and had actually been there..

Angel knew she couldn't stay there in case he returned. As much as she hated the idea of going to stay with her parents for awhile, but the idea sounded more appealing then returning to Druxel Manor and to James.

"He was asking all sorts of questions", Mrs. Hayes continued.

"Like what?" Angel asked.

"He wanted to know how long you had been back in town and if I knew when you'd be back."

Angel wondered how much longer it would be till he returned. She had to hurry and pack a few things and get over to her parents before he returned. "Thank you, Mrs. Hayes. I'd like to stay and talk, but I really must be going", Angel called as she ran towards her apartment.

"But . . . ", Mrs. Hayes called after her, but Angel kept on going.

She searched her apartment quickly for an overnight bag and went to her room with it. She grabbed whatever she could and quickly packed what she could find and grabbed her keys and purse.

Before Angel could get out the door, the phone rang. Angel sat her overnight bag down and grabbed the phone. It was Scott. "I can't talk now," she said breathlessly, "I need to get over to my parents house."

"Slow down," Scott said, just tell me what's going on."

"I don't have time now", Angel said and hung up the phone.

She grabbed her overnight bag and hurried out to her car. Angel had just pulled her car out on the road when her cell phone rang.

"Hello?"

"Angel, I need you to tell me what's going on", Scott said.

"Do you remember that man I told you about, the one who attacked me?"

"Yes, he hasn't attacked you again, has he?"

"No, but Mrs. Hayes just informed me that he's been to my apartment and he was asking questions about me."

"Oh no, Angel, I want you to come stay with me at my house."

"I don't think that would be a good idea, Scott."

"Why not?"

"I just don't. I think it's best if I go stay with my parents."

"Angel, don't argue with me."

"Scott, I can't stay with you."

"Listen, I'll come over to your parents after work and we'll discuss this then", Scott said before he hung up the phone.

13

Angel pulled up to the large double gates of her parents estate and came to a stop. The security guard opened the gates and waved her on through.

She pulled her car in the large garage before entering the house through the private entrance. Angel remembered the last time she had been home. It was a month or so back. Her father had hosted a huge party with a lot big business professionals. Their parents had been real disappointed when Trevor hadn't attended. Angel was getting tired of making excuses for Trevor's failure to attend family functions. She'd been doing it far too long.

Angel walked into the living room and sat her overnight bag on the sofa. She then walked over to the fireplace and looked at all the photographs lined up on the mantle.

She picked up a photograph and examined it. It was photograph of her and Trevor when they were children. Why couldn't things be as simple as they were then. Angel put the photograph back and picked up another. It was a photograph of Angel and Trevor the day they had come to live with the parkers. Angel sighed and placed the photograph back on the mantle. How could Trevor doubt their parents after everything they had done for them.

Angel didn't want to bother the hired hand. She was use to doing everything on her own now, so she walked back over to the sofa, picked up her overnight bag and carried it up to her room.

Her room was the same way she had left it the day she had left for college. A lot had happened since the day she had left for college. She had met Scott two weeks after leaving this room behind.

This was the first time she had been back to her room since she left for college. It seemed like just yesterday that she'd been in here. Angel sat down on her bed and looked around the room. Her posters still hung from the walls.

Angel unpacked her overnight bag before she picked up the phone and called her office. Harold was out of the office, so she left a message with his assistant, Karen that she was back in town and would be into work first thing in the morning.

As soon as she hung up, she called her father next. She hoped he wouldn't ask to many questions because she didn't have the answers for him. She wasn't ready to let to many people know that she was in danger.

If she was to tell her father about the man, he would be right up at Druxel Manor telling Trevor off. She didn't want to get her father too worked up.

Her father had been taking heart pills for the past six months. The doctor had told him he was under too much stress from his business and needed to start taking it easy, but her father had seemed to have forgotten the meaning of take it easy.

"Hi Daddy," she said as soon as he father came on the line, "How have things been going for you?"

"Better now that you're back in town and we know where you are. Why didn't you call us?"

"Now, Daddy, you know I would have called you if I could have, but it wasn't possible."

"I know Princess, it just worries me when I don't know where you are or who you're even with."

"I'm sorry Daddy," Angel said, "I truly am."

"You're forgiven this time, just don't make a habit of it, now was there a reason why you called?"

"Yes Daddy, I'm just calling to let you know I'm going to be staying with you for awhile."

"Why?" her father asked. "Now you're beginning to worry my."

"It's nothing Daddy," Angel lied, "My apartment is just getting sprayed for pests."

"Are you sure that's all it is?"

"Yes, Daddy."

"Alright, I believe you."

Angel told her father bye and hung the phone. She felt guilty. She had been telling a lot of lies since Trevor had sent her that telegram. Angel wished she would have hung up the telegram and had just ignored it.

****

Angel just finished putting her makeup on when the doorbell rang. She had already informed the hired hand that she wouldn't be needing their help during her stay here and that when Scott arrived, she would let him in.

Angel hurried down stairs and let Scott in and led him into her father's study where they could talk in private and not be disturbed. Angel had gone over and over in her mind what she was going to say to Scott, but she still wasn't prepared for what she was about to say to him.

As soon as they were seated on the sofa in the study, Scott turned to Angel, "Come home with me?"

This was going to be harder then Angel imagined. "I don't think that would be such a good idea."

"Why not?" Scott pleaded. "We have always talked about living together someday, why can't someday be now? Tonight?"

"Scott, if you would have asked me to move in with you a week ago, I would have said yes."

"Why can't you say yes now?"

"Because under the circumstances, it wouldn't be right?"

"What circumstances? Don't you trust me to protect you?"

"It's not that at all. The thing is, I made a decision this morning that I need to stick to and moving in with you now after making this decision wouldn't be right."

"What decision? Come on Angel, tell me what decision have you made?" Scott asked. Angel could hear the panic in his voice. She knew it was now or never.

"It's over, Scott", Angel said in a whisper.

"What was that?"

Angel spoke up a little louder, "I said it's over, Scott."

"What do you mean? What's over?"

"Us, Scott, our whole relationship is over."

"Please don't say that . . . ."

"I have to, Scott, it's the truth."

"But it doesn't have to be, I'm sure whatever it is, we can work it out."

"No, Scott, I don't want to work it out. I did something while I was out of town that made me realize I don't want to continue this relationship."

"And that would be?"

"Are you sure you want to know?"

"Come on, just tell me. I can handle the truth."

"I made love to another man", Angel said and looked away. She couldn't bring herself to look at Scott. She knew she had just hurt him deeply and did not want to see the hurt in his eyes.

Scott was silent for awhile before he spoke. When he finally did, he yelled, "You Bitch."

Angel winced as the tears began to fall. Angel had never

expected Scott to be so harsh. It hurt, but she deserved it. She had asked for it all.

"How could you cheat on me this way?" He demanded.

"None of this was planned, Scott.

"Are you trying to tell me that it just happened?"

"That's exactly what I'm trying to tell you", Angel snapped.

"Who is this guy anyway?"

"He's a guy that Trevor hired."

You're brother hired a man to have sex with you? I don't think I want to hear anymore.

Before Angel could say another word, Scott left, slamming the door behind him. Angel sat and sobbed. Breaking up with Scott was more painful then she ever imagined, but the fact still remained that she didn't love Scott. Not the way he deserved to be loved.

14

The next morning, Angel got up and went to work. She tried as hard as she could to forget everything that had happened the night before, but it was nearly impossible to do.

Angel sat staring at the computer monitor in front of her when Harold walked into the office. "So, did you get that story you were working on?" He asked.

"No, it didn't pan out."

Harold shook his head as he walked toward his office, "You're damn lucky, Angel, if you weren't my best reporter I'd have to let you go" He went in his office and closed the door.

A few moments later, he emerged from his office, "Angel, I'd like you to write an article about a bank robbery that took place last night," Harold said as he laid a file folder in front of her, "John Preston was supposed to write this article, but he had a family emergency to attend to."

Harold went back to his office. Angel picked up the file folder and began to leaf through it's contents. It had a few photographs and a bunch of notes John had taken. The robbery had taken place at a bank in Richmond Heights.

Angel's mind drifted back to the scene that had taken place in her father's study the night before. After Scott had left, Angel had cried herself to sleep.

Her father had come home and found her asleep on the sofa. Once he woke her up, he wanted to know what had happened. Angel told him about breaking up with Scott, but she purposely left out the part about James.

days began to turn into weeks and Angel threw herself into her work as much as possible to keep her mind off things. She missed James a lot and was even beginning to miss Druxel Manor, but after the way James had hurt her, she knew she could never go back as long as James was there.

Angel was beginning to experience many sleepless nights because she couldn't get the memory of James out of her mind. When she did manage to get some sleep, she dreamed of her and James making love to each other.

Angel was beginning to look like hell from lack of sleep. Her eyes were puffy and were beginning to turn black. Angel got up from her desk and poured herself a cup of coffee.

Angel had just down at her desk again and took a sip of coffee when she suddenly felt someone watching her. She looked up and saw James leaning in the doorway watching her.

No, she told herself, it couldn't be James. She had to be seeing things. Angel got up and walked over to a filing cabinet and began going through some files to try to take her mind off James.

Angel froze when a failure set of arms wrap around her and embrace her from behind. Angel knew without a doubt that it was James and it felt wonderful to be in his arms once again.

James turned Angel to face him and looked deep into her eyes before he tenderly kissed her. After the kiss he pulled her closer to him and Angel found herself laying her head on his shoulder.

"I love you", James whispered in her ear. Reality sank in at that moment and the hurt flooded her once again. Angel pushed James away. "Don't, it won't work this time."

"Angel, please come with me. I can explain the whole thing."

Angel thought about it for moment before she finally agreed to go with him. "Just let me take care of a few things and I'll be ready", Angel said.

Angel went into Harold's office and told him she needed to take the day off. He wasn't happy about it, but he reluctantly agreed. Angel quickly locked a file she had been going over earlier in her desk before grabbing her jacket and briefcase.

Without a word, Angel followed James out. The sun was shinning brightly, with very few clouds in the sky. A true sign that Spring was near. The warmth of the sun felt great on Angel's skin.

James opened the passenger side door of his car for Angel. After she was in, James walked around to the drivers side and got in. James turned to look at Angel like he wanted to tell her something, but instead he turned and started the car.

Angel remembered the last time she had been in James' car. It was the first day Angel had met James. That day seemed like a whole eternity ago.

James pulled the car into the parking lot of a coffee house not far from the newspaper office. James parked the car. He sat for a few minutes fiddling with his keys. He looked deep in thought for a moment before got out and came around and opened the car door for Angel.

They walked into the coffee shop in silence. The silence was causing Angel to feel miserable. Angel had never felt this uncomfortable around anyone her whole life.

Once they had their coffee and was seated at the table, Angel asked, "So how much did my dear old brother pay you to come after me?"   ˎ

"If you must know, your brother isn't paying me anything. In fact, your brother has no idea I'm even here. After you left, your brother no longer had any use for my services and let me go."

"And you expect me to believe that?"

"Yes, I do expect you to believe that."

"Why should I?"

"Because it's the truth, Angel," James said, "I know I don't have any proof right now, but Angel,, your brother misunderstood my intentions, when I made love to you, it wasn't to distract you, and it had nothing to do with the money your brother was paying me, I made love to you for the simple fact that I love you."

James seemed so sincere that a part of Angel deep down wanted to believe him.

James continued on, "I know we haven't known each other long, but we have been through so much together since we me, I love you, Angel."

Tears began to roll down Angel's cheeks, "I love you too, James."

James reached across the table and reached out and took Angel's hand in his. It felt wonderful. Angel wished she could make time stop and freeze this moment. forever, but she knew she couldn't.

15

They ordered another cup of coffee and Angel filled James in on everything that had been happening since she got back into town, including her apartment being trashed, Jake Taylors"s man coming around and asking Mrs. Hayes questions, and that she was now staying with her parents. She also told James about breaking up with Scott.

Angel noticed that James looked pleased when she told him about her's and Scott's break up, but there was no denying the look of disapproval on his face when she told him where she was staying. Angel hated the fact that James was still keeping a lot of secrets from her.

James offered to go with her and help her clean her apartment to see if anything was missing, so they quickly finished up their coffee and left the coffee shop. Before they went to Angel's apartment, they swung back by the newspaper office to pick up Angel's car, then James followed Angel to her Apartment.

They spent the rest of day at Angel's apartment and in the end found nothing missing. Angel wondered what they could have been looking for.

Angel called Detective Morgan, the officer who had came to her apartment the evening she reported the break in. Angel explained to Detective Morgan that nothing was missing, which meant this wasn't a robbery. Whoever had broken in, had come there looking for whatever they thought it was Angel had in her apartment, but didn't.

Detective Morgan promised to keep her informed if he found out anything new. Angel told James what the Detective had told her. James pulled Angel to him and hugged her. It felt so great to be back in James' arms. Angel never wanted what she now had with James to ever end, even if he was keeping a lot of secrets from her.

After Angel hung up the phone, she called a local Chinese take out and ordered in Chinese for dinner. After she hung up, she went and sat down on the sofa next to James..

I really wish I could convince you to go back to Druxel Manor with me", James said.

"I'm not ready to go back there and I really don't think I'll ever be ready to go back there."

"Trevor really does feel bad about what has happened, I'm sure things would be quite different if you were to go back," James said, "I think he has learned his lesson."

"Things won't be different though unless Trevor decides to tell me everything. I'm tired of all the secrets."

James began to massage Angel's shoulders. "Maybe Trevor will tell you everything if you go back."

Angel laughed, "You really don't know Trevor, he's not the type to give up that easily."

James began kissing the back of Angel's neck, then worked his way up to her ear and began nibbling on it. Angel's body began to tingle all over. Angel began to breathe heavier. "Are you sure we should be doing this?" Angel asked, "The Chinese food should be here soon."

Don't worry about it", James said right before he kissed her on the lips. He then began to massage Angel's breasts through her shirt. Angel's nipples became hard and erect. Angel's breast longed to be freed.

Angel reached the point where she hungered for more. She wanted to feel her flesh against James' flesh. She couldn't seem to get close enough to him. Their clothes were becoming a distraction.

Just then the door bell rang. They both pulled away, breathless. Angel felt disappointed because they had to stop. Angel closed her eyes and tried her best to steady her breathing.

"Wait right here and I'll get the food," James said, "You're going to need to eat to have enough energy for what I have planned for us later", he said with a wink and then went to answer the door.

Angel's breathing returned to normal. A few minutes later James returned with the food. Angel took one look at James and burst into laughter.

"What is so funny?" James asked as he set the food down on the coffee table.

"Your hair is a mess . . ."

"Gee, thanks a lot", James said as he began running his fingers through his hair, but only managed to mess it up more.

"You didn't let me finish", Angel said laughing.

"You mean you want me to let you finish poking fun at me?'

"And you have lipstick smeared all over your face", Angel said finishing what she had been saying.

A blush crept over James' face and then he began to laugh, "I wonder what that delivery guy thought."

"That's exactly what I was thinking", Angel said laughing.

"I'm glad you are finding amusement at my expense", He said as he reached over and messed her hair up.

Angel laughed as she got up from the sofa and headed into the kitchen.

"What are you doing?" James called after her.

"You'll see", she said.

A few minutes later Angel returned carrying two wine glasses and a bottle of wine she had remembered she had in the kitchen. She opened the bottle of wine and poured some in each glass while James opened the containers of Chinese food.

They laughed and talked as they ate. Angel was on her third glass of wine and was beginning to feel a bit tipsy. James laid down on the sofa and pulled Angel down on top of him.

At first they just talked, but before to long they were kissing. Angel slipped her hand beneath James' shirt and began to rub James' broad chest as they kissed.

James slowly unbuttoned Angel's shirt and ran his hands over her breasts through her black lacey bra.. Angel could feel heat searing through the lace under his touch.

John reached behind Angel and undid her bra. Slowly pulled the straps down and freed her breasts which were aching for his touch. Angel arched up to meet James' touch as he cupped each breast. As soon as his hands made contact with her breasts, Angel gasped.

James then bent his head down and flicked one nipple then the other before he turned his attention back to her mouth. As his lips met Angel's, her lips parted and his tongue slipped in.

Angel needed to feel her flesh against James, so she quickly unbuttoned his shirt and slipped it off from him without breaking the kiss.. Next she went for the snap on his slacks, but James stopped her.

"Slow down," James whispered, "I want to savor every moment of this." James rolled to the floor pulling Angel with him. This time James was on Top.

He kissed her once more on the lips, then he kissed each eye lid before he began moving down again. He nibbled on Angel's left ear and she shivered in delight.

He then began trailing kisses up and down her neck. He then moved lower to her breasts. He took one nipple in his mouth and sucked on it for a few minutes, then he moved to the other one. He alternated between the two for awhile. Angel wondered just how much more of this torture she could take. She had to have him in her.

"Make love to me", She whispered.

"I am," he whispered back, "Just relax and enjoy this."

Finally, James began to move down even lower. He was getting closer to the part of Angel's body that was aching for his touch the most. James pulled Angel's skirt up and began trailing kisses up and down her stomach.

James moved lower. Angel gasped as he began trailing kisses along the inside of her leg. Finally he slipped one finger then two under the elastic of her underwear and into her.

Angel moaned with pleasure as she arched her hips and his fingers slid in even deeper. Angel moaned through wave after wave that rippled through her body.

Angel reached up between them and began undoing his pants. This time James didn't stop her. Once Angel got them to his knees, James kicked them the rest of the way off, then he quickly took Angel's underwear off.

"I can't wait any longer", he moaned and within seconds he was in her. It wasn't much longer and they were both riding high on a wave of pleasure and moaning.

When it was all over, they both fell asleep tangled in each other's arms on the floor.

16

Angel was awakened by the sound of the phone ringing. It was dark outside. Angel got up and headed into her office to get the phone. She hoped it hadn't woke James up.

Angel answered the phone before sitting down. Angel yawned before speaking. "Hello?"

"There you are," her mother said, "Your father and I have been worried sick about you, why didn't you let us know you weren't coming back here to stay tonight?"

"Sorry, mom. I thought I was coming back there to stay before I left for work this morning, but my plans changed and I got so busy I forgot to call", Angel said in an almost whisper. She was trying not to wake James.

"Why are you talking so quietly? Is Scott there? Did the two of you get back together? That's it, isn't it? The two of you are back together . . . ."

"No, mom, we're not."

Angel's mother paid no attention to what Angel had just said to her and continued on, "That is wonderful, now you and Scott can attend your father's business party together tomorrow night and the town picnic on Saturday."

"Mother, didn't you just hear a word I said?" Angel said, getting irritated.

"No dear, what did you say?"

"I said Scott and I are not back together. I do have a man here, but it's not Scott."

"Oh!" She said, sounding surprised by Angel's words, "Who is he? What's his name?"

"He's a friend of mine. His name is James."

"How long have you known him?"

"I met him the last time I was out of town."

"Well, bring him to the party tomorrow night. I would like to meet him and sure your father would too."

"We'll try our best to be there."

More like check him out, Angel thought after she hung up the phone. Angel stood and walked out into the hall. She ran right into James who had come looking for her.

"What were you doing?" he asked.

"My mother called. We're invited to my father's business party tomorrow night."

"I hope you said no. You did say no, didn't you?"

"Why shouldn't we go?"

"Just forget I said anything, if it mean's that much to you, we'll go."

Angel knew James was hiding something. All these secrets were really bothering Angel. She wished she could get James to open up and tell her, but she knew that wasn't going to happen anytime soon.

The last thing Angel wanted to do was fight with James again, so all she said was, "That's sweet of you."

"So you want to go?"

"Yes, my parents are expecting us, and they want to meet you."

"Don't you mean they want to check me out?"

Angel laughed. She was starting to realize how much her and James thought alike. She felt as if she had known him forever.

****

James and Angel had spent the rest of the night in her bed. Angel yawned and stretched and then shut her eyes again. Suddenly they popped back open. She realized she was late for work.

She quickly untangled herself from James and got out of bed as fast as she could. In the process, she woke James up. He looked startled when he asked, "What's going on?"

"I over slept and I'm late for work."

"I wish you would call in sick."

"I wish I could, but I've been messing up a lot at work and I really don't want to lose my job."

"I know, I understand."

Angel realized something. James had not mentioned a job in the time Angel had known him and he didn't seemed worried about getting to work. "Tell me something James, what do you do for a living?"

"That's confidential", James said.

Angel laughed, "No, seriously, what do you do for a living?"

"I am being serious. My job is confidential."

Another secret, Angel thought. All these secrets James was keeping were really starting to hurt Angel's feelings. She was beginning to feel that James didn't trust her.

Angel shrugged the feeling off and headed into the bathroom for a shower. When she came back out, James was sitting on the edge of the bed talking to someone on the phone.

"She'll be there just as soon as she can", James said to the person on the other end of the phone line and glancing in Angel's direction. The phone must have rang while she was in the shower.

James hung up the phone and Angel turned and walked into her walk in closet to pick out an outfit for work. James followed her in and started trailing kisses along her neck.

"Not now," Angel said giggling, "I have to get ready work." Angel grabbed a blouse and skirt with a matching jacket and walked back out into the bedroom.

James followed her back out into the bedroom. "I really wish you wouldn't go to work today."

"I know, but I have to go."

"And just what am I supposed to do all day while you're gone?"

"Oh, so that's why you don't want me going to work today", Angel said laughing.

"You've got me all figured out," James said with a grin, "I guess I can't pull one over on you, can I?"

"No, you can't, I'll see right through you every single time."

Angel quickly got dressed. She only had enough time to throw on her clothes and tie her hair back with a ponytail holder. She had no time to put makeup on.

"How about I swing by the newspaper and take you out to lunch today?" James asked as Angel was rushing out the door.

"You're on. You can pick me up at one, but remember, I have to be back to the office afterwards."

****

Harold was in a bad mood when Angel showed up and she didn't blame him. She had been messing up quite a bit lately. As soon as Angel arrived, he called her into his office.

"This is not like you, Angel,?" Herold yelled, "Now I demand to know what's going on?"

"I wish I knew, Sir, but I don't."

"Come on, Angel. You have to know something. First you disappear, then you call and tell me you're working on a story, but when you return, you don't have a story for me. Now you're taking off from work early and showing up late," Harold yelled, then lowered his voice, "What's up with this Sir business? How many times have I told you to call me Harold? It makes me feel old."

"I'm sorry, Herold. I really am. Not just for calling you Sir, but for everything. I'll try harder and I promise, as soon as I find out what's happening I'll let you know."

"I'll forgive you this time, but please do not make it a habit."

"I won't, Sir . . . Uh, I mean Harold", Angel said as she backed out of his office."

Angel was relieved once she made it to her desk. Angel picked up a stack of memos and began shuffling through them until she came to one about a local fund raiser taking place, which meant Angel would need to leave her office.

Angel picked up the phone and dialed the phone number on the memo. She spoke with the organizer of the event, a young woman about meeting that afternoon to get pictures and more information about the fund raiser

Angel read through the rest of the memos. From the looks of it, today was going to be a long day. Angel hated it when she had to work late, but she had messed up so much lately, there was no way she could get out of it. After Angel checked her phone messages, the day proved to be an even longer day then she had thought.

Then Angel remembered her father's business party. Her parents would really be hurt it they didn't attend. This meant Angel needed to be home no later then four. Angel realized that as much as she hated to do it, she had to cancel her lunch date with James. If she didn't, she'd never get any work done.

Angel picked up the phone and dialed her phone number. She was beginning to worry that James wasn't going to answer the phone when he finally did answer.

"I hate to do this, but I need to cancel our lunch date."

"Why? I was really looking forward to seeing you."

"I know, I just have so much work to do, but I'll try to be home by four."

17

Angel's lunch consisted of a bag of chips and a can of soda she had gotten from the vending machines. She plugged away at her work as she ate.

Soon it was time for her to leave for her meeting with the organizer. Angel had just got in her car and got her safety belt on when her cell phone rang.

Angel retrieved her cell phone from her briefcase wondering who would be calling her on her cell phone now. Her parents never called her during working hours unless it was an emergency. It must be James, she thought as she answered it.

"Hello, James?"

A man on the other end of the line laughed. It was a laugh that made Angel nervous. "Who is this?" Angel demanded.

The man laughed again before speaking, "You'll find that out when we meat for the first time which won't be too long from now."

"When we meat? I don't even know who you are, so I doubt I'll be meeting you anytime soon. How did you get this number anyway?" Angel demanded sounding more tough then what she actually felt.

"All you need to know at this time is that I'm watching you. I know your every move and we will soon be together."

"Who is this? Angel demanded again. The line went dead. The man had hung up on her. A chill went through Angel as she started her car. What did he mean he was watching her every move and they'd be together soon? Angel wondered.

Was this guy just bluffing to scare her, or was he for real? Angel hoped he was just bluffing to scare her. The thought of someone watching her made her nervous.

Angel found herself jumpy and looking in every direction as she drove to make sure she wasn't being followed. The thought of someone attacking her while she was alone wasn't a very pleasant thought. There wouldn't be anyone around to help her. Maybe James was right to worry about her going to work.

Angel had to talk to Harold about getting some time off, but she wondered what she would tell him. She just couldn't come right out and tell him she was in danger or could she? Angel thought. But then again, she'd messed up so much, maybe right now wasn't a good time to ask for some time off.

She thought about talking to James about all of this, but worried he would over react. I'll have to come up with something later, Angel thought as she pulled up in front of the small office where she had agreed to meet with the woman.

Angel sat in the car a few minutes pulling herself together. That call had really shaken her up. Maybe he dialed the wrong number. That had to be it, Angel thought trying to reason with herself.

Angel took a deep breath and then stepped out of the car. When Angel entered the office, she was greeted by a man who showed her to another smaller room to wait.

OUN

While Angel waited, she thought about the call she had received and decided it best to get things over with as quickly as possible and get back to her apartment and to James.

When the woman finally came in, Angel asked questioned and collected the photos the woman had promised on the phone. Twenty minutes later, Angel was back in her car with all the information she needed.

No matter how hard Angel tried to convince herself it was a wrong number, she just couldn't. Too many strange things had been happening lately for it to be a wrong number. There was no doubt in Angel's mind that the man had dialed the right number.

Angel got her cell phone out of her purse and dialed her phone number. James answered on the first ring. "Is there something wrong?" James asked.

"No, I'm just calling to let you know I'm on my way home now", Angel said. She felt guilty for lying, but she wasn't sure if she was ready or not to tell him about the call she had received.

Angel hung up and then started her car. Hearing James' voice made her feel a little better, but she knew she'd feel a whole lot better once she was home and in James' arms.

****

Angel was relieved when she pulled up in front of her apartment building. Since the phone call, she still couldn't shake the feeling that she really was being watched.

Angel walked as quickly as she could to her apartment. She couldn't seem to get inside fast enough. As soon as she opened the door, she went straight to James who was sitting on the sofa reading the newspaper and collapsed right in his arms.

"There is something wrong. Now tell me what it is", James demanded

"Nothing is wrong," Angel said, "I just missed you."

"Are you sure that's all it is?"

"Everything is just fine", Angel said as she pulled James on top of her and kissed him.

"If you keep this up, we're never going to make it to your father's business party," James said.

Angel had completely forgotten about her father's business party. Since Angel received the phone call, it was about all she could think of. "I could really use a bubble bath", Angel murmured.

"One bubble bath coming right up", James said as he stood and left the room before Angel could respond.

Angel could hear James rummaging around in her bathroom and then the water come on. A few minutes later he came back out. When Angel tried to stand up, James stopped her. James scooped her up into his arms and carried her into the bathroom.

Once in the bathroom, he sat her down on the toilet and proceeded to take her clothes of from her. When he had her completely nude, James scooped her up in his arms once again and sat her in the tub that was filled with bubbles.

James then proceeded to give Angel massage. It felt wonderful. She hadn't realized her muscles were so tense until James began working the muscles in her shoulders and neck.

Angel closed her eyes and began to relax. No man had ever done anything like this for her. Angel realized that she enjoyed being pampered like this.

Twenty minutes later, James lifted Angel out of the tub and carried her into her bedroom and laid her on the bed. "Wait here, don't move", James said before leaving the room. A minute later he returned carrying a large towel and began to towel her dry from head to foot.

Once Angel was completely dry, James kissed her before having her sit up. Once Angel was sitting up, James set about the task of getting her clothes.

First he got her bra and underwear out of her dresser and brought them over and put them on her. He went over to the walk in closet and went inside and then came back out and asked, "Which dress would you like to wear?"

"My spakley blue evening gown", Angel answered, wishing her parents would have gave her more time so that she could have shopped for a new dress for the party.

Once Angel was dressed, Angel set about doing her hair and makeup while James sat on the bed and waited. Angel realized that James didn't have anything to wear to the party. "James, what are you going to wear to this party? We can cancel if you'd like."

"No, there's no need to cancel, don't worry about a thing."

Just then the doorbell rang and James excused himself to go answer the door. Angel could hear him talking to someone and then thanked them. She wondered what James was up to.

A few minutes later James returned, carrying a tuxedo. He laid it out on the bed. "I'm going to go get a shower", James said as he turned to go out.

"No, wait", Angel said.

"What is it?

"I want to return the favor and help you get ready for the party."

"No, no, no," James said, "You'll mess your dress up and I don't want you to do that on my account."

Angel looked down at her dress and realized that James was right, "Okay, but remember, I owe you one."

18

Angel and James arrived a little early and guests were already beginning to arrive. After James handed his keys to the parking attendant his keys, Angel led him around to the private entrance.

The house was alive with maids rushing around trying to get everything ready for the big event. All of Angel's father's parties were big events with the best of everything and her father always saw to it that things were perfect and everything ran smoothly.

Angel led James into the formal dining room where the guests who had already arrived were enjoying a drink before dinner. Angel's parents came rushing up to them.

Angel's mother laid one hand on James' shoulder, "You must be James?"

Angel's father extended his hand and shook hands with James, "It's so nice to meet you. Just relax and enjoy yourself."

After Angel's parents moved on to greet some of the other guests, Angel and James found there seats and sat down. Angel looked up and gasped.

"What's wrong?" James asked.

"I can't believe my parents would do this to me!" Angel exclaimed. Her eyes were glued to the entrance. James followed her gaze. Her eyes were fixed on the guy who was entering and had stopped to talk to Angel's father. Angel's father laughed at something Angel's father had said to him.

"What is it? What's wrong?" James asked, puzzled by Angel's reaction.

"I can't believe they would invite Scott here when they know we are no longer together," Angel said. "I have this feeling my parents are up to something."

"What do you think they're up to?"

"I have a feeling they are going to try to get me back with Scott", Angel said before she excused herself to go to the ladies room.

Angel went into the bathroom and checked her hair and makeup. When she was done and was leaving the bathroom, she noticed the door to her father's office was open and the light was on.

That's strange, Angel thought. Her father always closed and locked the door to his office when he was hosting a party. He must have forgot that he left the light on and the door open, Angel thought, but as she got closer, she could hear voices coming from inside the office. Who could be in his office? Angel wondered.

Angel moved closer to the door so that she could hear it was and what was being said. "We can't do anything until that James fellow is out of the picture." Angel froze. It was Scott's voice.

"But if we don't act quickly . . ." Another man said.

Scott interrupted him, "We have to do things my way, or the whole plan could fail."

What was Scott up to? Angel wondered. Was he plotting to get her back? Just then James came out of the dining room. "There you are," He said, I was getting worried when you didn't return", he said.

The conversation in the office came to a stop. "Shhh . . ." Angel said as she pulled James off to the side and pushed him up against the wall and kissed him.

Angel could feel Scott watching them as him and the guy he'd been talking to left the office, closing the door behind them. Angel didn't break the kiss till she knew that Scott and the man had gone back into the dining room.

"What was that all about?" James asked.

"I'll explain later", Angel said, as she took James by the hand and led James back into the dining room where they were getting ready to serve dinner.

Dinner consisted of grilled duck breast in a wild rice crepe. Dessert was a lemon custard tartlet, her father's favorite dessert. When Angel finished her dinner, she sipped her glass off wine.

The maids began clearing up the dishes and everyone started heading into the ballroom. This was Angel's favorite room in the house as a child. She used to come into the ballroom and daydream of the day she'd be able to attend her father's parties.

The day finally came shortly after her sixteenth birthday. Angel remembered she had dressed so carefully for that night. She had spent weeks shopping for the right dress.

Angel felt like she was on top of the world when her father's business partner's son, Rick Hudson had asked her to dance. She had a crush on him for years. She had been heart broken when she found out he had a girlfriend.

Angel walked around introducing James to everyone she had known her whole life. Most of them had become like family to her. While Angel did this, she tried not to pay much attention to what Scott was doing, but she couldn't help noticing him hanging around the bar. He seemed to really be putting the liquor away.

Angel began to become concerned. She had never seen Scott drink this much. He had always been a light drinker. Angel wanted to help him, but what could she do? They were no longer a couple. It's really none of my business, Angel thought, trying to convince herself.

Angel noticed out of the corner of her eye, that Scott was leaving the bar area and heading in their direction. Oh no, Angel thought. This could mean trouble.

"So you're the guy who stole my woman?" Scott asked, his words were slurred from all the drinking he had done.

"No one stole me away from you, Scott", Angel said. "I left of my own free will.

Scott acted as if he didn't hear Angel, if he did, he must not have believed what she had said. He was moving closer to James. Angel noticed look on Scott's face. She could tell he was angry.

"Scott . . . ."

Before Angel could get another word out, Scott swung and hit James in the right eye, knocking James to floor. Angel gasped. Scott stumbled backwards and then turned and walked away.

Angel bent over James, "Are you alright?" she asked.

"I think so", he said as he stood up.

Everyone had stopped what they were doing and gathered around Angel and James. Angel's parents pushed their way to the front of the crowd. "What happened?" Angel's father asked.

Angel explained the whole thing to his parents. "How dreadful!" Angel's mother exclaimed.

"I will definitely have a talk with that young man just as soon as I find him," Angel's father said. "I will not tolerate that type of behavior in my home", as he turned and walked away to go search for Scott.

"Are you sure you're okay?" Angel asked.

"Yes, I'm a little shaken up, but I'll be fine."

Shortly after that, Angel and James left the party and headed back to Angel's apartment.

19

James drove in silence on the way home. Angel was deep in thought. Something just wasn't right with Scott. Scott wasn't being himself, well at least the Scott Angel knew.

The Scott Angel knew rarely drank and he never got violent the way he did tonight. Maybe I misjudged Scott all this time, Angel thought as she leaned her head back against the back of the seat and closed her eyes.

"Hey," James said, interrupting her thoughts, "Just what was going on tonight when I came looking for you when you didn't return from the restroom?"

Angel opened her eyes and looked at James, his eye was swollen and had turned black, "It was nothing,," Angel said, "Don't worry about it."

"Angel, I know something was going on, now please tell me what it was."

Angel told James the whole story about discovering the light on in her father's office, and what she had overheard Scott and the other guy saying.

James looked deep in thought for a moment before he responded, "So you think Scott is plotting to get you back?"

"Yes."

"Are you sure there wasn't much more than that?"

"What do you mean?" Angel asked.

"Are you that's what they meant, or do you think you could have misunderstood and that it could have been something much bigger they were talking about?"

"No, what else could it have been?" Angel asked in a sarcastic tone of voice.

"Forget I asked that," James said. "You're right, it couldn't have been anything more."

Angel could tell that James didn't truly believe what he'd just said. Angel began to wonder if her brother had told James something about Scott. Whatever it was, it couldn't be true. Trevor had hated Scott from the moment Angel had introduced them.

Jaimes' secrets were really starting to get to Angel. She had to bite her tongue just to keep from telling him how much his secrets were bothering her..

James looked deep in thought the rest of the way home. Angel sighed and closed her eyes to rest them and to think the rest of the way back to her apartment.

****

Morning came quickly and James and Angel got up early to get ready for the annual town picnic. It was a perfect day for it. The sun was shining brightly and there wasn't a cloud in the sky.

Angel rushed about packing their picnic basket while James was off getting his car washed. James eye was looking much better this morning. A lot of the swelling had gone down and his eye wasn't so black.

James returned and seemed to be in a real good mood. He even a bit playful this morning. When they had firs got out of bed, he had chased her through the apartment When he had caught her, he had pushed her down on the couch and tickled her. After that, James had made love to her.

James gave Angel a quick kiss before taking the picnic basket from her. Angel grabbed a blanket that she had sat on the couch earlier and followed James out the door, locking it behind them.

When they arrived at the park in the center of town, families were already starting to arrive and finding places to lay down their blankets. Off to the side was a stage where a band was setting up.

Angel looked around. She couldn't see her parents anywhere, but she wasn't worried. Her parents were usually late to everything, except for things that involved business. When it came to running the family the family business, they were very prompt.

Angel and James found a spot a few feet from the stage. James sat everything down, then took the blanket and spread it out on the ground. Once they were seated on the blanket, Angel pulled James to her and kissed him. They were interrupted by someone clearing their throat.

Angel and James pulled apart. Angel looked up to see her sister, Karen. Karen looked at James and then gave Angel a confused look, which meant she hadn't talked to their parents lately. "Sorry to interrupt the two of you, but do you mind if I sit here with the two of you?" She asked.

"Not at all, have a seat", Angel said.

Once Karen sat down, shot Angel a look. It was a look that Angel had seen Karen give this look many times while growing up. It was the look Karen always gave her when she wanted Angel to spill it.

"Karen, This is James," Angel said, then turned to James, "James, this is my sister, Karen."

James reached over and shook Karen's hand, "Nice to meet you."

"Nice to meet you too", Karen said before standing up. She reached down and took Angel's hand and pulled her to her feet. "You and I need to have a talk", she said.

"I'll be right back", Angel told James as Karen pulled her aside

"What is going on?" Karen hissed. "Who is this James guy you are with and why were you kissing him? Where's Scott?"

"Scott and I broke up", Angel said.

"Why?" Karen demanded.

"Because I discovered I'm not in love with Scott."

"And you think you love this guy?" Karen asked looking in James' direction.

"No I don't think I love him," Angel snapped back at her, "I know I love him."

"Come on Angel, please don't be mad at me," Karen said, "I'm just concerned and don't want to see you getting hurt."

"I'm not going to get hurt", Angel said, as she turned and walked back to the blanket. Karen followed her. When they got back, their parents were there. Their mother was spreading out a blanket next to their blanket.

Angel sat back down next to James. She looked up and saw Scott a few feet away talking to some men. This was going to be a very long day.

At that same moment, Karen looked up and saw Scott also. Karen gave their parents a hug and then started walking in Scott's direction. What is she up to? Angel wondered.

Angel watched as Karen struck up a conversation with Scott. Every once in a while they would turn and look at Angel. Angel was hurt. She wondered how Karen could betray her wishes that way. Karen wasn't even giving James a chance.

Angel stared at Karen and Scott. James noticed and looked over in the direction Angel was looking. "What's wrong?" James asked.

"Just a little sisterly betrayal", Angel Answered. "She might as will have stabbed a knife in my back."

20

The band started to play. It was a really great band and Angel was really enjoying the music. Karen had come back over to the blanket and was acting as if nothing happened.

Between songs, Drew Hammond, the town mayor got up on the stage and announced that the children's games would be starting in ten minutes. all the children rushed off in the direction the mayor had indicated.

The band began to play once again and Angel sat sipping a soda pop. Karen turned to her and asked, "What's wrong?"

"As if you don't already know."

"No, I don't know. If this is about Scott . . . ."

"Of course this is about Scott. What were you talking about with him?"

"We were just having a casual conversation . . . ."

"Yeah, a casual conversation about me."

"I admit, your name came up", Karen said.

"It more then came up. You went over to Scott to talk about me specifically with him.

"Okay, I admit it. I'm just worried about you, Angel".

"I know this is a personal conversation," James said, "But why are you worried about Angel?"

"Well, uhh . . ." Karen said, trying to think of an answer.

"I'm just fine," Angel Said, "I don't need you to worry about me." Angel got up and walked in the direction the group of children at the far end of the park.

All the children were split into age groups. They were preparing for the first event which was a gunny sack race. Angel felt James come up behind her and wrap his arms around her.

"Try not to let things get to. Everything will work out just fine in the end. I want you to just relax and enjoy yourself today."

Angel didn't know what it was, but James always managed to make her feel as though all was right in the world. "You're right, maybe I am taking things too seriously", Angel said as she leaned back against James' chest.

The gunny sack race began and the first set of children took off. Other children on the sidelines cheered for their friends. A little blond curly haired boy came up in the lead and won. The little boy was handed a blue ribbon and all the other children received ribbons. The child with the most blue ribbons in the end would win the trophy.

As the children all got ready for next event, Angel and James went and sat down on a near by bench. They could hear the sound of the children laughing all around them. The world seemed perfect.

Angel knew that the world around her was far from perfect. She was in danger and she had no idea why. Trevor had stirred up some sort of trouble. Angel couldn't figure out they, why they were after her and not Trevor.

"Want another soda?" James asked, jolting Angel from her thoughts.

Angel turned and smiled at James, "Sure".

Angel watched as James got up and walked in the direction of the blanket and her family. Angel jumped when her cell phone rang. Who would be calling me now? Angel wondered. Just about everyone she knew were here at the picnic.

Angel too her cell phone out of her shorts pocket. She answered it and put it up to her ear. "Hello?"

"So we speak again", the man said. It was the same man who had called the night before.

"What do you want?" Angel asked.

"Just checking in and reminding you that we are watching you", the man said.

"I don't believe' you," Angel said bravely, "I think you're bluffing."

"My sources tell me that you are at the town picnic, sitting on a bench at this very moment".

There was a click and Angel knew he had hung up. Angel was frozen with fear and was still holding the phone to her ear when James returned with her soda. "Who are you talking to?" James asked looking around, "I thought everyone in town was here right now."

"They are, I was just talking to someone who had a lead in the next town over," Angel said, "But it's not something that has to be taken care of now though."

"That's good. You should be relaxing and enjoying yourself, not working", James said.

"Your absolutely right," Angel said as she shut her cell phone off before sticking it back in her pocket, "There, no more disruptions".

"At least not from the phone, but with all these people here, I think it's safe to say that there will be more disruptions before the day is over."

****

Lunch time finally arrived. Lunch consisted of fried chicken that Angel had fried up that morning, corn on the cob, and watermelon that Angel's parents had brought with them.

Angel took one last bite of her watermelon. She was stuffed. Angel and James helped her parents and her sister clean up everything from the picnic.

When they were finishing up, Scott came up to Angel's father and tapped him on the shoulder. He whispered something in Angel's father's ear and he got up and followed him.

Angel watched as they both walked over to a guy in a suit. Angel noticed the look on James face, as he watched them too. Angel had a feeling James knew who the guy in the suit was by the way he was looking at him. The look on James' face was a look of shock.

"James, what is it?" Angel asked, "Do you know that man?" Angel had only met the man a few times herself while growing up. She use to play with his son J.C. when she was a little girl. How could he possibly know this man? Angel wondered. "James, are you okay?"

James snapped his attention back to Angel. "Oh yeah, sure. I'm just fine. Don't worry."

"Are you sure?" Angel was finding it impossible to believe James. He seemed shaken up when the man who had worked for her father before she was even born.

"Of Course I'm sure. They're getting ready to start a softball game for the adults. lets go play, it'll be a lot of fun."

James seemed to be really enthusiastic about it, so Angel agreed to play. She got up and followed him to the other end of the park where the softball game was scheduled to be.

Angel felt that James' decision to play in the softball game had something to do with him wanting to get away from her father's employee so that he wouldn't see him. Why doesn't he want the guy to see him? Angel wondered.

21

When the game was over, Angel and James walked over to the cooler and they each took out a can of soda from the cooler and sat down on the blanket. Angel was surprised that her father hadn't yet returned. She wondered what could possibly be going on. It wasn't like her father to leave during a family get together. Now that they had all grown up, their time together was valuable and her father understood this, that was why, even when there was a business emergency, he had one of his employees take care of it.

Karen was a few feet away, talking to some of her friends she had grown up with. Angel was surprised to see Susan Thomas there. It was rumored around town that her father had a heart attack and was in the hospital. Word had it that they didn't expect him to live too much longer. She thought for sure that Susan and her family would be up at the hospital with her father.

What also surprised Angel was the man Karen was standing beside and was holding hands with. It was her high school sweet heart, Justin Myers. They had broken up the Summer after graduation. Neither one them had liked the idea of a long distance relationship and with them both going off to separate colleges, they felt it was best. Everyone was surprised because everyone had expected Karen and Justin to marry someday. Angel couldn't wait till she could talk to Karen about this. Angel and probably half the town would be thrilled if Karen and Justin got back together.

The thing about Angel and Karen was that whenever one got upset at the other for something the other did, the anger never lasted long. It had been this way for as far back as Angel could remember. Angel and Karen had always been best friends. It was Karen who had taught Angel how to apply make up. They told each other secrets and revealed who they happened to have a crush on to each other. Karen had always been more then just a sister to Angel.

Angel caught movement out of the corner of her eye. Her father was sitting at a picnic table just a few feet away with Scott and the same man he had been talking with earlier. They seemed to be in a heated conversation about something. Angel had to hear what they were saying, but she had to do it in a way they wouldn't know she was around. Angel thought quickly. She excused herself, telling her mother and James that she needed to use the restroom.

Angel walked in the direction of the restrooms, but once she was out her mother's and James' view, she circled around and hid behind a huge Oak tree not far from where they were sitting at the picnic table. She could hear everything they were saying clearly. "We need to catch Jake Taylor at his own game", her father was saying. "Are we even sure it is Jake Taylor?" Scott asked. Now how do my father and Scott know who Jake Taylor is? Angel wondered.

Maybe it's just a coincidence that my father knows Jake Taylor, Angel thought, Maybe he's just a business acquaintance of my father's, but the next words out of her father's mouth, told Angel that she was mistaken. "Whatever we do, we must stop Jake Taylor from getting anywhere near Angel". Now how did he know about all of this? Angel wondered. Someone came up behind Angel, Angel was so startled that she let out a little yelp and a firm hand quickly covered Angel's mouth.

Angel turned to find out who had grabbed her. It was James. "You nearly gave me a heart attack," Angel hissed at him, "What about my mother, does she know you followed me?"

"I don't think she even noticed I even left", James whispered.

"What do you mean?" Angel Whispered back.

"she was having girl talk with Karen when I got up and came looking for you," James whispered.

Angel remembered what she had been doing before James had came up and startled her. She turned her attention back to her father, Scott and the man. Her father was getting up from the picnic table and walked in the direction of the blanket where her mother and April were sitting. A few minutes later he returned. "Okay, you guys ready? It's all set", her father said. Scott and the man stood up and they walked in the direction of the parking lot. What's going on? Angel wondered. This was not like her father.

Angel turned her attention back to James. "My father, Scott and that man know Jake Taylor", Angel said. Angel could tell by looking at the expression on James' face that this was not news to him. James already knew this information. "Well, well, well, it appears I unearthed one of his secrets, Angel thought to herself.

****

When Angel and James returned to the blanket, Angel was surprised to see Justin sitting next to Karen on the blanket. Before sitting down, Angel introduced James and Justin to each other. Angel made a mental note to call Karen later after they returned home.

"Where's dad?" Angel asked casually.

"Oh, your father had an emergency at the office that only he could deal with", her mother said. Angel could tell by her mother's tone of voice when she said it, that she was disappointed that her father had left.

A frisbee came flying over and landed on their blanket. Angel looked around to see where it came from. The owner of the frisbee was a little boy. Angel picked up the frisbee and tossed it back to the little boy.

"Thank you ma'am", the little boy yelled before running off to play again.

The sun was starting to go down and it was beginning to cool off. They all decided to call it a day, so they packed up their stuff. Karen volunteered to take their mother home on her way home.

Angel watched as Karen said bye to Justin. "I'll call you sometime this week", Justin promised Karen before leaving. Angel had a feeling that it wouldn't be the last time Karen and Justin got together. Something was definitely beginning to blossom again between Karen and Justin. Angel could just feel it.

22

The next few weeks passed by quickly. Angel worked harder at work and put in extra hours to make things up to Harold. Angel spent her lunch breaks with James. The evenings were spent at home, or they went out to eat. A couple of nights they had even gone out dancing. Angel was having more fun then she could ever remember having in her life.

They had plans that night to meet Karen and Justin at a local restaurant for dinner. It was now official. Karen and Justin were back together. It was just like old times again. Karen was more accepting of Angel James' relationship and had even apologized to both James and Angel for the way she had acted.

Angel was just getting ready to leave the office when her cell phone rang. Please don't let it be Karen saying she's canceling, Angel said under breath as she answered the phone.

"Hello?"

"It's so nice to hear your voice again." It was the mysterious male caller again.

"What do you want?" Angel asked in a firm tone of voice.

"We'll be seeing each other face to face real soon."

"What do you want with me?"

"You'll find that information out real soon", he said before hanging up.

Angel stuffed her cell phone into her purse, then grabbed her briefcase before heading out the door. The parking lot was nearly empty. Once Angel was in the car, she took a quick look around. Angel spotted a car parked right across from hers. It was a silver colored car and Angel could see a man sitting in the drivers seat. He was looking in her direction.

Angel locked her car door before starting the car. Once she got her car started, the driver in the silver car started his. The man waited till Angel pulled out, and then he pulled out. Angel fumbled in her purse for her cell phone just in case she needed it. Angel saw a traffic light up ahead and knew she had to stop.

As soon as Angel's care came to a stop, the silver car came to a stop right behind her, but instead of the driver waiting for the light to change, he opened his door and got out and started walking toward her car. Angel was shocked when she saw that the man was a man who worked for her father. He was the one she had seen the day of the picnic talking to her father and to Scott, but something didn't seem right. The look on his face frightened Angel.

Just before he got to her car, Angel decided to floor it. She pushed on the gas as hard as she could and the car took off at full speed. Angel remembered she was holding her cell phone and was glad she had her number on speed dial. She looked behind her, and could see the man in the silver car was right behind her and gaining speed. It seemed like forever before James answered the phone. "James, I'm so glad to hear your voice. I was beginning to think you weren't there."

"I just got out of the shower. Is something wrong?"

"I need you to be out front waiting when I pull up", Angel said.

"Why? What's the Matter? Where are you?"

"I don't have time to answer your questions right now, but can you go out front right now and wait for me."

"Sure", James said before hanging up.

Angel could see her apartment complex straight ahead. She hoped James had made it outside. Angel was relieved when she saw James standing by the curb. The tires squealed as she came to a stop. The man in the silver car had begun to slow down, but once he saw James, he sped up again and took off as fast as he could.

Angel jumped out of the car. she ran to James and hugged him as tight as she could. James wrapped her in his arms and embraced her. "I can't believe he did that", James said.

Angel pulled away from him for a moment and looked James square in the face. "Do you know that man?" Angel asked him.

"Why don't we go in the house. I think it's time I told you everything. We can also plan what we're going to do, but we can't stay here. It's not safe."

Angel followed James into the apartment. Part of her was glad she was about to find out everything, but another part of her was afraid of what she was about to learn. She knew it couldn't be anything good. If it was, Trevor and James wouldn't have gone to such great measures to keep it from her.

Once they were inside the apartment and seated on the sofa, James spoke, "It's hard for me to figure out just where to start. I guess you might want to know first off, who owns Druxel Manor, wouldn't you?"

"Yes, just who does own Druxel Manor?"

"You do."

"No, I'm serious, who owns Druxel Manor?"

"I am being serous, you own Druxel Manor", James said.

"If I own Druxel Manor, just how did I become the owner?"

"You inherited it from your biological parents."   ,

"So it belongs to Trevor and I?"

"No, Druxel Manor is all yours. Your biological parents felt at the time they wrote their wills, that you would benefit from it more then their sons would."

"Sons? You must be mistaken. Trevor and I don't have a brother."

"Angel, do you remember Dave, don't you? You met him right before you left Druxel Manor."

"Yes."

"He's your brother, Angel. That's why he told Trevor about the two of us. He was only concerned about you, his little sister."

"You mean he really is Trevor's twin?"

"Yes, he is. There is more I need to tell you. I told you the good things first. The rest is bad."

"What is it? Does it have anything to do with Jake Taylor?"

"Yes, but it also has to do with your adoptive parents and this part isn't easy to tell you."

"What about my parents?" Angel asked.

"It's about the adoption."

"What about our adoption?" Angel asked. She was getting an uneasy feeling in the pit of her stomach. She knew that what James was about to tell her about her parents wasn't anything good.

"The adoption wasn't a legal adoption."

"What do you mean it wasn't legal? I have seen mine and Trevor's adoption papers."

"The adoption papers you saw were fake", James said.

23

Angel was silent for the longest time before she said, "No, that can't be true. It just can't be."

James got up and left the room. A few minutes later he returned holding a notebook. "It's all right here", James said as he handed it to her.

Angel took the notebook from him. As soon as she opened it, she burst into tears. She knew that what James was telling her was the truth. She recognized the hand writing right off. There was no mistaking, it was Claudia Parker's hand writing.

Angel began reading what was in the notebook. It was step by step plans to kid nap Trevor, Dave and Angel. The plan included, in Claudia's own words, to knock off their parents. They had hired Jake Taylor to do the kid napping and to kill their parents. Some how the plan did not go according to plan because they never got Dave. Angel closed the notebook and handed it back to James. She felt sick to her stomach.

"Are you alright?" James asked.

"Not really", Angel said laying her head back on the sofa.

"Would you like to lie down?" James asked.

"No, I think I'm going to be alright. I want to know the rest like where you fit into all this and why someone has tried to nab me more then once and why I have been receiving the phone calls."

"Phone calls? What phone calls are you talking about?" James asked.

Angel realized she hadn't told James about the phone calls.

"Why didn't you tell me?" James asked when Angel finished telling him.

"I didn't want to worry you. I knew if I told you, you'd be worried and see to it I didn't return to work."

"Of course I would, Angel and that's just what I intend to do. You are in danger."

"Why am I in danger?"

"Jake Taylor turned against Pete and Claudia once he learned about the wills your parents had left behind listing you as the one to receive your parents fortune."

"Fortune?" Angel asked.

"Yes fortune. You have money sitting in several bank accounts that became yours on your eighteenth birthday, plus several assets like stocks and bonds. Jake Taylor, being the greedy man he is, has decided he wants your inheritance and he would do anything to get it from you, including murder."

Angel swallowed a large lump that had formed in the back of her throat. Things were worse then she thought. You still haven't answered the question I asked you earlier out front. Do you know that man who was driving the silver car?"

James looked away for a moment, then looked back at Angel, "Yes".

"How well do you know him?" Angel asked, afraid of what the answer might be.

"Angel, I can't keep this from you any longer. I have been wanting to tell you this from the moment we met. I'm J.C."

"J.C.?"

"Don't you remember me?" James asked.

"Of course I remember you, but why did you tell me your name was James?"

"My name is James. J.C is short for James Colby, but everyone calls me James now."

"I thought Trevor hired you?"

"He did. I'm a private investigator."

"You went against your own father?" Angel asked in amazement.

"Yes, I didn't want to, but I don't agree with a lot of the stuff he does."

"If he works for my dad, well for pete, why did he come after me tonight?

"I hope I'm wrong about all this, but I honestly think he's started working for Jake Taylor."

Angel looked at the clock. They were supposed to meet her and Justin in an hour. "What about Karen?" Angel asked, "Is she in on this?"

"I don't think so. I doubt she even knows what her parents have done, but to be on the safe side and meet them for dinner. Just in case she does know, we need to act as normal as possible. Once dinner is over we need to get back here and pack. We're leaving tonight."

"Okay", Angel said. She was left with no other choice but to go along with him. She knew he was just trying to protect her. "Are we going back to Druxel Manor?"

"No, they'll find you there. I need to get you out of the state. I'll make the arrangements while you're in the shower and getting dressed."

Angel got up and gave him a hug. "Is it okay if I call you J.C.?" She asked.

"Sure", he said.

"I love you J.C."

I love you too Angel", James said and then he kissed her before she went off to take her shower.

When Angel finished her shower and returned wearing a black dress, J.C. was just getting off the telephone. "Everything's all set", he said.

"Where are we going?" Angel asked.

"That's a surprise. All I can tell you for now is that we are

going by private plane so that we don't leave a paper trail. A friend
of mine owed me a favor and is letting us borrow his private plane."

Angel was still in a state of shock. She had no idea how she was
going to make it through dinner without Karen getting suspicious,
but she knew she had to. What worried Angel was the fact that
Karen knew her better then anyone. It wouldn't be that hard for
Karen to realize something was wrong.

"Are you sure you wouldn't like to just cancel our dinner plans?"
Angel asked.

"Why should we cancel?" James asked.

"I was just thinking that if we go through with the dinner
plans, Karen will figure out something is wrong. I have never been
able to keep a secret from Karen. She knows me like an open book."

"We have to go through with the dinner plans."

"Why?"

Because Karen and Justin are probably already on their way to
the restaurant and if we leave now and don't show up, Karen may
get worried and call Claudia and Pete who just might get suspicious
and track us down before we even have a chance to leave the airport.
If we have dinner with Karen and Justin as planned, we'll be able
to leave without alarming anyone.

Angel knew James had a point, so she agreed to the plan.. She
would just have to pull herself together enough to keep Karen
from getting suspicious of them.

Angel grabbed her evening bag and they headed out the door.
When they arrived at the restaurant, Karen and Justin were already

there. Seeing them together was like old times. Angel wished she could share in their happiness, but after what James had told her tonight, she wasn't even sure if she could trust Karen.

Karen stood up and gave Angel a big hug as soon as they got to the table. She seemed really happy. Angel had always known that Karen and Justin were meant for each other. They had always seemed so perfect together and Angel had always hoped that she would find the same kind of happiness they shared with each other when she got older.

"Is there something wrong?" Karen asked as soon as they were all seated at the table, "You seem really stressed out about something?"

"It's just work and all the extra hours I have been putting in, I guess it's just all starting to catch up with me", Angel said. She hated lying to Karen. She hated lying to anyone period. Honesty had always been a virtue that Angel valued in herself.

Angel was relieved when the dinner was over. She couldn't remember ever lying so much as she had just spent doing to keep Karen from getting suspicious of them.

Angel and James went straight back to her apartment and began packing everything they feel she would need. An hour later, James called to confirm the plans and to make sure the plane was ready. They got back into the car and James drove them to the airport.

24

The flight to Florida went quick. A limousine was waiting for them when they stepped off the plane. Once in the limousine, Angel asked James, "Where are we going?"

"The same friend who owed me a favor, Kevin Miller, he has agreed to let us stay with him at his estate while we're here. If we checked into a hotel, we could be tracked down."

Angel laid her head back against the seat. She was tired and found herself fighting sleep. Soon she could no longer fight it. Her eyelids were feeling heavy. Before drifting slowly off to sleep, she laid her head on James' chest.

****

The next morning Angel awoke and yawned and stretched. Then she remembered the events that had taken place the night before. and slowly opened her eyes. She was alone in a large king size bed. James must have carried me in last night, she thought as she looked around the extremely large room. It made Druxel Manor look small in comparison. Angel was still not over the fact that she owned Druxel Manor.

The reason Angel had decided to move into her apartment instead of buy a large mansion like her father's was because she had decided she wanted just the simple things in life. Sure, Angel enjoyed living in a large mansion with maids, but once she graduated college, she felt she needed a change of lifestyle.

Now she had a big decision to make once of this was over. She had to decide then, whether to move in to Druxel Manor or to remain in her small one bedroom apartment. Mrs. Hayes had become to feel like a grandmother to her, and if she chose to move into Druxel Manor, she would miss Mrs. Hayes a lot, even if she could talk a persons ear off with her long stories. Angel couldn't help but laugh. Some of Mrs. Hayes stories did seem to be a little off the wall at times.

Angel heard a noise and turned to see James entering the room. He was wearing just a robe and looked as if he had just stepped out of the shower. "Good morning sleepy head," said, "It's about time you woke up."

"Why, what time is it?" Angel asked, yawning.

"It's 10:34 AM., James said, pointing at the clock on the night table beside the bed.

"Oh my," Angel said, sitting up, "I need to go take a shower."

"Not quite yet," James said pushing her back down on the bed and kissing her, "We have all day for that", James whispered in her ear before he began trailing kisses down her neck.

Angel felt her body automatically respond to James' touch. She found herself withering underneath him with desire. When James kissed her on the lips again, she kissed him back hungrily. When she tried to undo his robe, he stopped her. James pushed himself up off the bed and excused himself as he went into the bathroom. Angel could tell by the smile on his face, that he was up to something.

When he returned, he was still smiling as he pulled the covers back and scooped Angel up into his arms. "What are you doing?" Angel asked, laughing. •

"You'll see, James said. Then he kissed her. Angel returned his kiss with an urgency she had never felt before with any man.

James broke the kiss and carried her into the bathroom. There was no window. The only thing lighting the room was the soft candle light from the candles James had lit a placed around the large sunken tub.

Angel was already nude. James had taken off all of her clothes when he had taken her to bed. James set Angel down in the tub. Then he removed his robe, before getting in with he.

He soaped Angel up, taking his time when washing her breasts. He also took his time washing the lower part of her body as well. Angel returned the favor of bathing James and taking her time in just the right areas.

When they finished bathing each other, James got out and helped Angel out of the tub. Then they dried each other off. "Wait here", James said as he left the bathroom. Angel wondered what he was up to. He was gone for the longest time and when he returned, he was caring a blind fold. After James put the blind fold on Angel, he scooped her into his arms and carried her into the bedroom.

Angel could smell roses as soon as they entered the bedroom. Angel was curious to know what James was doing. She didn't have to wait long to find out. James removed the blind fold. He had covered the bed with light pink rose petals. No moment had ever been more perfect then this very moment.

James carried Angel over to the bed and gently laid her down on the rose petals. He made love to Angel that made her feel loved and cherished. Afterwards, James called downstairs to the kitchen and had the bring brunch up to their room.

A maid brought up bacon, eggs, toast, a bowl of fresh strawberries and a pot of coffee. As they ate they talk about how life was for both of them while they were growing up and they discussed what had influenced Angel to go into journalism. Angel realized that James never told her what he did for a living, so she asked him again.

"I might a well tell you", James said, surprising Angel, "I'm a private investigator. I own my own private investigating company."

"Why don't you have to work right now?" Angel asked.

"I'm on vacation. I took some time away from the business to come spend some time with you."

A sad thought came to Angel's mind. She realized that her time with James wasn't going to last. James would soon be returning to his business and their time together would soon be coming to an end.

"What's wrong?" James asked, when he noticed the sad look that crossed her face.

"I just realized our time together will soon be coming to an end."

"What do you mean, our time is coming to an end?" James asked, "I have no intentions of ending our time together any time soon. One of the perks of owning my business is the ability to be able to make time for you, which I intend to do."

Angel smiled and wrapped her arms around James and kissed

him. They made love one last time before deciding to get dressed for the day. "I wonder what your friend thinks." Angel said, while they were dressing."

"About what?" James asked.

"About us staying in bed most the day."

"He doesn't know."

"What do you mean? How can he have not noticed we aren't up yet?"

"He's out of town. Except for the hired hand, we have the house all to ourselves until next week while he's away on an important business trip."

What does he do for a living?" Angel asked out of curiosity.

"He's a lawyer."

"Have you enlisted his legal services? Is that how you know him?" Angel asked.

"Oh no, he's one of my clients. He has hired me to work on several cases with him over the past five years and from that, a friendship has developed between the two of us."

Angel and James quickly finished dressing and Angel got her first glimpse of the house as they headed down stairs.

25

At the bottom of the stairs, the floor was marble. When they climbed the one step the went up to the raised living room, Angel knew right away that James' friend was into art. He had several expensive painting hanging on the walls and several sculptures in the room. The furniture was all done in brown leather.

"This is really impressive", Angel said.

"If you think this is impressive, come with me and I'll show you something even more impressive, follow me", James said as he turned walked back out of the room.

Angel followed James, wondering what he was going to show her. They walked down a long hall, when they got to the end, he opened the door. James took Angel by the hand and led her into the room. The room was pitch dark inside and Angel couldn't see a thing. James flipped a switch and the room flooded with light. Angel's mouth hung open in amazement at what she saw.

She was standing in the middle a theater. She had always wanted a private theater for her and her friends when she was a teenager and her father could have afforded to put one in, but he firmly believed that TV. and movies were not a good way for teenagers to spend their time. He had raised Angel to be well rounded and most of her spare time was spent doing extra curricular activities. She was not only on her school's tennis team, but she was also on the debate team.

"Would you like to see a movie?" James asked.

"Sure, if it's possible", Angel said.

"Wait right here then", James said, as he turned and walked away. Angel watched as James went up a flight of stairs and into a little booth. He picked up the phone and punched in a number. After a few minutes he hung up the phone. As he hung up the phone and came back down the stairs, a man entered the room. James spoke with the man for a few moments. Then the man went up the flight of stairs and James walked back to where Angel was standing.

"It's all set", he said, as he took her by the hand and led her to a seat up in the very front.

After they sat down, Angel turned to James and said, "This is my first time.."

"What do you mean this is your first time? What are you talking about?" James asked.

"This is my first movie. I have never been in a movie theater before."

"Are you serious?" James asked.

"Yes I am", Angel said. She was little embarrassed about the whole thing.

"Why haven't you been to a theater before?" James asked, sounding a little shocked by what Angel had just told him.

"My father would not allow it when I was growing up and the opportunity never came up until now", Angel said.

The lights dimmed and an old black and white movie came
on the screen. About fifteen minutes into the movie, Angel could
feel James watching her. She turned to look at him. After awhile,
they both couldn't keep their eyes off each other. Soon the movie
was completely forgotten and they were making out. Angel could
not believe this was happening. Making out with a guy in a movie
theater had been a fantasy she had when she was a teenager. Now
over ten years later, the fantasy was coming true.

When the movie finally came to an end about two hours later
and the lights came back on, Angel laughed. She had no idea about
James, but she had no idea what the movie was even about.

The man came out and said, "I hope you folks enjoyed your
movie".

"Oh, we sure did, Roger," James said, "Thank you."

"Anytime folks", Roger said as he headed out of the room.

So far Angel had the best day of her life and wondered what
was in store for the evening. She was sure she would find out soon,
and whatever it was, she would love it.

When they got back to their room, Angel was surprised, there
was an evening gown and a tuxedo laid out on the bed. They put
the clothes on, then Angel did her hair and her make up. James
picked up the phone and made a quick call before he took her by
the arm and led her downstairs.

When they arrived out front of the house, the limousine was
waiting. The chauffeur was standing there with the back door open.
Once James and Angel got in, he closed the door and went around
and got in.

Angel was surprised when they got to the restaurant. It had to be the most expensive restaurant in town. The atmosphere in the restaurant was great. A man with a violin walked around and paid soft music while everyone ate.

When they finished eating, James paid the bill and they left the restaurant. Angel expected the evening to be over and for them to head back to the house, but the evening wasn't over yet. James had one more surprise for her.

He took her to a real public theater. They bought their tickets. Then they stopped at the stop bar and loaded up their arms with popcorn, candy and soda pop before entering the theater. After tonight, I'll need a good work out, Angel thought. She wondered if there was a gym near by where she could go to work out. She made a mental note to ask James about it later.

They sat down just before the lights dimmed for the movie to start, but just before the lights dimmed, Angel thought she saw a failure face. I have to be seeing things, that couldn't possibly have been Scott, he doesn't even know we are here, Angel thought to herself.

The movie started and Angel pushed the thought that she saw Scott to the back her mind and turned her whole concentration on the movie. The movie was a comedy and Angel and James laughed all the way through it.

When the movie ended and the lights came back on, Angel couldn't help but turn and look where she had thought she saw Scott. There was no one there. Angel was relieved.

As soon as they exited the theater, the limousine pulled up and the chauffeur got out to help them into the limousine. It had been a long, but wonderful day and Angel was tired. She stretched and yawned.

"So did you enjoy your day?" James asked.

"Yes I did, I enjoyed it so much that I wish it didn't have to end so soon, but I know that it has to because I'm so tired", Angel said, yawning again. Angel laid her head against James' chest. Before she knew it, she was sound asleep.

26

The next morning Angel awoke to find James on the phone talking to someone. "Are you sure you can't find someone else to take care of this?" James asked the person on the other end of the line. "No that fine, I'll be there as soon as I can."

James hung up the phone, but before Angel could find out what was going on, James picked up the phone and dialed a number. He lowered his voice, so Angel didn't have a clue as to who he was speaking to.

As soon as he hung up, Angel asked, "What's going on?"

James jumped and turned around and looked at April. "Oh, you're awake, I thought you were still asleep. How long have you been awake?'" James asked.

"Long enough to figure out you're going somewhere", Angel said.

"Look, I wish there was a way I could stay here with you, but there has been an emergency at my office that only I can deal with, but don't worry, you won't be alone here for long."

"What do you mean?"

"I called Trevor, he said he's on the next flight out here", James said.

"I wish you would have talked to me first before you asked him to come here", Angel said.

"Who else was I supposed to call?" James asked, "Trevor is the only one we can trust right now and there is no way I'd even consider leaving you here alone."

"Why would that be so bad?/" Angel asked, "No one knows we're even here."

"I have to take the next flight out, that could leave a paper trail to where you are and I can't risk you being here alone."

Angel realized he had a point. She was actually scared, but she wasn't about to let James know. Another thought crossed her mind, What if this was it? What if she never saw James again? Angel tried to push the thought to the back of her mind, but she couldn't stop the tears that began to slowly roll down her cheeks. She tried to hurry and wipe the tears away as quick as she could, but she wasn't fast enough.

"What is it?" James asked.

"It's nothing", Angel said. She didn't want James to know how worried she was.

James put his arms around Angel to comfort her, "Don't give me that, come on now? You can tell me."

"I was just thinking that this could be it and that we might not see each other ever again."

"Why wouldn't we?" James asked, "I'm not even taking all my stuff with me."

"I just thought that you would get busy with work and forget . . ."

"I am never going to forget you Angel, and I will be back, you have my promise", James said.

Angel threw her arms around James, "I'll miss you, but I trust you, and I know you'll be back", she said, before she kissed him.

"I'm glad you trust me," James said before he got up and went over to the closet. He got out a suit and began dressing. Angel climbed out of bed and helped James with his tie.

James got out his suitcase and began to pack his clothes. Angel sat down on the bed to watch him pack. "I'll try to be back in two to three days, if not sooner", he said.

When he finished packing, he picked up the phone and arranged for the limousine to meet him out front to take him to the airport. Before he left, he came over to Angel, "God I'm going to miss you," he said, "Remember that I love you and I will be back, that's a promise."

"I love you too", Angel said. James kissed her and then he was gone. Angel began to miss him as soon as the door closed behind him. She knew he'd be back, but she still felt lonely without him there. She had gotten so use to him being there with her.

Angel thought of the best cure for her loneliness. She remembered that she needed to find a fitness center. That should take my mind off from the loneliness, Angel thought.

She looked in the nightstand drawer and found a phone directory. It didn't take long to find a fitness center about a block away. She realized the limousine would not be available, so she quickly dialed the number for a cab. She realized she would need to go to the mall to shop for workout clothes before she could go to the fitness center.

Angel hurried in and took a quick shower, then came out and put on a fresh clean pair of jeans and a royal blue tee shirt. She was just slipping on a pair of shoes when she heard a honk. She looked out the window to see the taxi had arrived.

Angel grabbed her purse and headed out. She knew she should tell someone she was going out, even though she knew she really shouldn't, so that they could tell Trevor when he arrived, but she knew that Trevor would just come and get her.

The mall was just opening when she arrived. She asked the cab driver to wait for her. She knew she needed to hurry because the meter was running, so she stopped and checked the store directory. She located a fitness shop and quickly headed in the direction of it.

In the fitness shop she was able to find everything she needed. She quickly picked out several workout outfits and a pair of aerobic shoes. On the way to the checkout counter, Angel stopped and grabbed a sports bag to store her workout stuff in.

There was three other customers in front of her in line. The store had not been open long, so there was only one sales person working the counter. When it was Angel's turn, she quickly paid for her purchases with her credit card. Then she quickly walked back out to the taxi and instructed the driver to drive her to the fitness club.

It was hot outside, so Angel was relieved when she walked into the fitness club because it was air conditioned. The cool air felt great on her skin after being out in that hot sun.

27

Angel was greeted at the front counter by a bubbly, cheerful blond. She helped Angel with the sign up forms and then had another woman, a brunet, by the name of Bridget, show her around the facility. The tour ended in the locker room.

Angel found her locker. She sat down on the bench and picked out one of her workout outfits and put it on. Then she put on her aerobic shoes. When she finished, she stored her street clothes, shoes and the rest of her workout outfits in her locker and then went out.

She found a beginners aerobic class that was just starting and joined in. When she was finished, she was drenched in sweat. She looked at her watch. It was after one. Trevor was probably already in Florida.

Angel went up to the juice bar and ordered a tall glass of orange juice. A guy came and sat down at the bar on the stool next to hers. He was an older gentleman with streaks of grey going through his hair.

He looked Angel up and down, "Well, well, well," he said, "What do we have here? You sure are a beauty."

Angel blushed, "Thank you", she said. She quickly finished her orange juice and headed for the locker room. She took a quick shower before she put her street clothes back on.

She stored her workout stuff in her locker. She went and found a pay phone and called the house. Ten minutes later the limousine arrived. When the chauffeur came around and opened the door for her, she expected to find the limousine empty. Part of her was surprised. I should have known, Angel thought as she got in.

"Why did you leave without telling anyone you were leaving or where you were going?" Trevor asked as soon as the chauffeur shut the door, "Do you realize how worried about you I have been? I thought Jake Taylor and his men had found you."

"I'm sorry," Angel said, "I didn't mean to worry you or anyone else."

"Well maybe you'll think next time", Trevor snapped.

"I didn't know I needed you're permission or anyone else", Angel snapped back at him.

"Come on, lets not fight," Trevor said, "I've been wanting to talk to you."

"Yeah, about what?" Angel asked.

"I'm sorry", Trevor said.

"Sorry about what?"

"About that whole thing with you and James in the end. I thought he was taking advantage of you. It was a complete misunderstanding and I realize now that I made a mistake and it was none of my business. I'm still learning to understand that you are an adult now and those kind of decisions are your's to make, not mine."

"You're right," Angel said, "Those are my decisions to make, no one else's, and I forgive you."

Trevor smiled and gave Angel a hug, "I'm glad to see the two of you hooked back up after you both left and if the two of you wants to be in a relationship, you have my blessing."

"Thank you," Angel said, "That means a lot to me coming from you."

"Just promise me one thing", Trevor said.

"What's that?" Angel asked.

"I know you think I'm really over protective of you, but from now on, can you let me know you're going to the gym or anywhere else. I want to go with you", Trevor said.

"I promise, but on one condition, you don't follow me around all the time."

"It's a deal", Trevor said.

****

The next two weeks flew by, with Trevor and Angel going to the Fitness club to work out every morning. The man who had spoken to her at the juice bar her first day there seemed intimidated by Trevor and never approached her, although Angel had caught him watching her from a distance a few times. The man made her nervous.

James was still not back from his trip, but he did call Angel almost everyday. Angel had just spoken with him the night before. He had told her that the situation in the office was beginning to clear up and that he might be able to return in a few days. Angel missed James, but tried to keep busy.

They were getting ready to leave when Trevor received a phone call from a friend of his that lived in New York. Angel waited for him to hang up so they could go. About thirty minutes later he hung up the phone. "Great news", Trevor said as soon as he hung up the phone.

"What's that?" Angel asked, a bit annoyed at the fact they were late leaving, which meant she was late for her aerobic class.

"You know the boat regatta that's coming up this weekend?"

"Yes", Angel said, starting to show some interest. Angel and Trevor had been trying to get tickets to it, but had no luck because it had been sold out.

"I just got us two tickets to this weekends boat regatta", James said.

"How did you pull that off?" Angel asked.

"My friend I just spoke with, he has a business partner who had two tickets, for him and a date, but as it turns out, the can't go after all, so my friend got the tickets for me. They'll be delivered by a messenger some time this afternoon."

When they finally made it to the Fitness club, the aerobics class was just about over, so Angel decided to use a treadmill for her daily workout. Trevor was only a few feet away, lifting weights.

"So we meet again", said a man.

Angel jumped and whirled around to see the man she had seen at the juice bar her first day. He must not have seen Trevor, or Trevor's presence no longer bothers him, Angel thought.

"I'm sorry I startled you", he said, "My name is Steven Kestler."

Angel glanced in Trevor's direction. She was relieved to see Trevor walking in their direction. "Nice to meet you", Angel said. Before the man could say another word, he looked up and saw Trevor heading towards them. He began to act nervous. "I need to be going", he said and was gone before Trevor got to them.

That was strange, Angel thought. "Was that man bothering you?" Trevor asked when he reached her.

"Not really," Angel said, "But he was sure acting strange though."

"What do you mean by strange?" Trevor asked.

"He saw you coming, and left as fast as he could. It was like he was trying to avoid you."

28

The next day, the day of the boat regatta, Angel talked Trevor into going to the fitness club, before heading to the boat regatta. Most everyone in town was at the boat regatta already, so there wasn't many people at the fitness club.

Only Angel and one other woman showed up for the aerobic class, so it was canceled. Angel had to settle for the treadmill once again, but today she didn't mind. She was too excited to mind. Angel was excited because she had never been to a boat regatta before.

Angel was a little worried about one thing though. James hadn't called her, but she figured he had just gotten real busy and didn't have time to call her.

When Angel was finished on the treadmill, she went into the locker room. The locker room was empty. Angel stripped off her sweaty workout clothes and grabbed a towel before heading into the shower.

The water felt good running down Angel's body. She was enjoying the feeling when she thought she heard a noise outside the shower. Either it's my imagination or one of the other members has entered the locker room, Angel thought, trying to convince herself.

Angel quickly finished up her shower. She wrapped a towel around her before getting out. She looked around, but no one was in sight. The locker room was still empty. They must have went out, or it's just my imagination, Angel thought.

Walked over to the bench in front of her locker and dropped her towel. Angel heard another noise and froze. The sound came from behind her. Angel turned around and came face to face with Scott.

"Scott? What are you doing here?" Angel demanded, as she grabbed her towel and wrapped it back around her.

Scott replied in a calm voice, "So you thought you could run from me."

"How did you find me here?" Angel asked, trying not to let her voice tremble.

"You didn't answer my question", Scott said.

"I'm not running from you, our relationship was over, long before I even left."

"Did you really think you could just end our whole relationship that easily after everything we have been through together?" Scott asked.

"Scott, you're really starting to scare me now", Angel said.

Scott acted as if he didn't hear what she had just said.

"Together, you and I can have it all and I'm not letting you get away from me that easily," Scott said, "I'm here to claim what is mine and you belong to me, Angel. We belong to each other."

"I told you already, Scott, you and I are finished. What we had was great at the time, but I don't love you and I'm not sure I ever loved you to begin with, I only thought I did", Angel said. "I'm not your's. I do not belong to you."

"You're wrong," Scott said, you'll always belong to me."

"No, you're the one who's wrong Scott. I have moved on. I'm with James now.

"I knew you would put up a fight," Scott said, as he took a rag out of his pocket, "You leave me no other choice, Angel."

Angel looked for an escape. She decided to try to run for the door, but didn't make it. Scott caught her and wrestled her to the ground. Angel tried to scream, but couldn't. The last thing Angel remembered, Scott had placed the rag over her nose and mouth.

****

Trevor had seen Angel go into the locker room over thirty minutes ago and she still hadn't returned. He was beginning to worry about her. He decided it was time to go in and search for her.

Trevor entered the women's locker room to find it empty. "Angel", he called out, but got no answer. It was apparent she was gone. He noticed the door that led outside in case of an emergency was open. He also so a rag laying on the floor.

Trevor walked over and picked up the rag and smelled it. He quickly went out the door. He saw Scott dragging Angel, who appeared to be unconscious into his car.

"Hey!" Trevor yelled, as he ran toward the car, "Stop!" But he wasn't quick enough. He grabbed a pen and paper from out of his pocket and quickly wrote down the license plate number.

Just then his cell phone rang. "Hello?"

"Hey, Trevor, this is James. Where are you two right now? I'm back in town and I can't wait to see Angel."

"I wish I could tell you for sure where she is, but I can't", Trevor said.

"What do you mean?" James asked.

Trevor told James what had just happened.

"I'm on my way. Call the police."

As soon as Trevor hung up, he called the police. They were sending a couple of officers right out. All Trevor could do was sit and wait. Trevor wished there was more he could do.

The ten minutes it took for the police to arrive seemed like an eternity. Trevor told them everything he knew. Shortly after that, James arrived. He looked really distraught. Trevor could tell just by looking at James, that he really did love his sister.

Trevor gave the police Scott's license plate number and they promised to do everything they could to find her. He hoped they found her soon. The police told Trevor they would call him at the house if they found out anything. The only thing they could do was head back to house and wait.

Trevor didn't feel that he could handle the wait. He wanted desperately, to begin searching for Angel himself, but he knew he would be more help by going to back the house.

Besides, he wouldn't know the first place to begin. The last thing he wanted was to mess up the police investigation and to put Angel in any deeper trouble then she was already in. If Angel was to get hurt in any way and it was his fault, he wouldn't be able to live with himself.

29

When Angel Awoke, she found herself tied and gagged in a motel room. The room was quiet. She looked around the room, but could not see Scott anywhere.

Angel jumped when she heard a noise. She looked up to see Scott coming in the door. He was carrying a brown paper sack. He closed the door behind him and came over to the bed and sat down. "Good, you're awake", he said.

Angel tried to talk, but couldn't because of the gag. She was relieved when he reached up and took the gag off from her. "You're an animal", she yelled.

"You don't really mean that", Scott said.

"Yes, I do, now let me go", Angel demanded.

"And risk you getting away from me again," Scott said, "I don't think so. This time we are going to be together forever."

"You are one sick man," Angel said, "I don't know what I ever saw in you. I don't even know who you are anymore."

"That's not true," Scott said, "I'm still the same person I have always been. I have not changed one bit."

"Then I really misjudged you because I thought you were a kind and carrying man", Angel said.

"I still am", he said.

"No you're not," Angel said, "There is nothing kind and carrying about what you are doing right now."

"One day, you will thank me for this, I can guarantee it", he said.

Scott opened the paper bag and began taking containers of Chinese food and placing it on the bed. "I hope you're hungry," Scott said, "Because I plenty of food here", he said.

"Don't even bother," Angel said, "I'm not hungry."

****

James and Trevor had been at the house for about an hour. They still had heard no word about Angel. A million different scenarios about what was happening to Angel right now were flashing through his mind. All of them bad.

"There's something I haven't had a chance to tell you", James said.

"What's that?" Trevor asked.

"I finally got the evidence to put them all away once and for all", James said.

"You mean you kept working on the case after I let you go?" Trevor asked.

"Sure, I didn't do it for the money, I did it for Angel" James said.

"You you really do love my sister, don't you?"

"Yes I do. I have never met anyone like Angel before," James said, "She makes my life feel complete. I don't know what I'll do if they don't find her."

Trevor could tell that James was being honest. He hoped that Angel was okay and that no harm had come to her. He knew Angel deserved the kind of life that James could offer her. "What kind of evidence did you find?" Trevor asked.

"I finally found the final plans and the contracts that were issued by Pete and Claudia Parker to Jake Taylor and signed and dated by all three of them. It's enough to give the FBI to make an arrest."

"Why haven't you contacted the FBI yet?"

"I just got the evidence this morning when I was preparing to leave," James said, then I called you because I wanted to present the information to you and Angel first."

"So what are you waiting for?"

"I'll contact the FBI just as soon as Angel is found and is safe."

****

"Come on now", Scott said as he tried to coax Angel to eat."

"I told you I'm not hungry", Angel said as she turned her head away from him.

Just then there was a thump against the door. Angel and Scott both turned towards the door as the door was kicked in. Several police officers came rushing into the room. Scott was too stunned to move. An officer hand cuffed Scott and led him out of the room, while another officer undid the ropes that were holding Angel captive.

Two officers stayed behind and took a report of what happened. A few moments later, Trevor and James came rushing in. Angel was surprised to see James.

James rushed over and hugged Angel. It felt great to be back in James' arms. For awhile there, Angel had wondered if she would ever feel James' arms around her again. Angel looked up and saw two men wearing suits standing in the doorway.

One of them stepped forward and asked, "Is there a James Morgan here?"

James stood up and walked over to them. "I'm James Morgan", he said.

"Hi, I'm agent Prescott and this is agent Phillips," he said, "We hear you have something we might be interested in."

Angel watched as James took a manilla envelope from his Jacket pocket and handed it over to the agent. The agent opened it and took out several papers and documents. She wondered what they were and why the FBI would want them.

"As you can see, all the proof is there", James was saying.

"We'll get right on this," agent Presscott said, "We'll contact you as soon as possible, is there a number where you can be reached?"

James gave them the number to the house and they left. Angel was relieved once they were out of the motel room. On the way back to the house, James explained to Angel what was in the manilla envelope. Angel was relieved. She'd soon be able to move on with her life. She only hoped that James would be a part of her future.

About two hours later after they returned to the house, the call they were all waiting for finally came. When James hung up the phone, he had a smile on his face. "It's all over", he said.

"What happened, Trevor asked.

"They caught them all," he said, it appears Scott worked for Pete Parker, but a few months ago, he started working for Jake Taylor behind Pete Parker's back."

Angel was shocked. She had trusted Scott with all her heart. "What about Karen?" Angel asked.

"She knew nothing about any of it", James said.

Angel was relieved. Trevor left the room to go make some business calls and James and Angel were finally alone at last. Angel wrapped her arms around James.

"We really need to talk", James said.

"About what?" Angel asked, fearing the worst.

James looked into Angel's eyes, "About our future", he said.

"What about it?" Angel asked.

"Will you marry me?"

Tears filled Angel's eyes, "Yes, I'll marry you", she said. She had never been so happy in her life. Her future was finally starting to look bright and Angel was looking forward to her life with James and Duel Manor.

Printed in the United States
732100002B